Knot My Valentine

M.P. Starkweather

Phoenix Eclipse Publishing

I want to dedicate this book to my two biggest fans, my husband Josh and my son Thom, who will probably never read any of my books. Thanks for pushing me to chase my dream. I love you both to the moon and back.

Acknowledgments

I would like to thank:

My Alpha and Beta Teams who try hard to keep me on track;

My Editing Team who does their best to make sure my books make sense and have as few typos as possible;

My Cover Artist, PC Designs, who's responsible for the gorgeous images on the front of this book

and My ARC Team, who catch some of the things the rest of us miss.

Contents

One

Small Town Life

COURTNEY

I wake to the sun streaming through my curtains. A moment of panic races through my mind, then I remember that I don't have to get up at sunrise anymore. I set my own hours now. I take a deep breath and count to ten. Letting my eyes scan the room, I ease myself into the realization that I'm home. This isn't the city, and I know that I'm safe.

A shudder works its way up my spine as the memory takes over. It's dark, my eyes refuse to focus, and a man stands over me. I know I've been drugged, and that I can't stop what's happening to me. I feel helpless and cry out for help.

No. I'm not there. I push the memory aside, climbing out of bed. I'm in the safest place I know. I've been here for three weeks now. Home. Miller Falls, Indiana, will always be home.

No matter how far I ran or how hard I tried to get away. Yeah, I enjoyed studying computers and technology in New York, but there was no way I could stay after what Chad did. And now I'm home. I can be me again. I decide on a quick shower before I go to work, thinking about the town and coming home as I get ready. Pushing those dark thoughts away and focusing on the here and now.

The town of Miller Falls, Indiana, has fewer than one thousand people living in it at any one time. I can tell you the intimate details of Ms. Gertrude's fight with her sister, Mr. Ross' falling out with his son, and the date Katie went on last night. How? Small town gossip. It's the one thing every small town has in common. I do my best to stay away from it, but when you work odd jobs for a living, it's impossible not to hear it all.

Now, that's not to say living in a small town is all bad. When anyone has trouble, we come together like family. When Kevin's house burnt down, the entire town banded together and rebuilt, refurnished, and redecorated him right back home in less time than anyone in a big city could have. I'm really not sure why I left in the first place, except that I got a full-ride scholarship to that tech school in New York. I've managed to settle right back into small town living in just a few days.

It's definitely a balancing act. And one I'm not very good at sometimes. My parents retired to Florida, but threatened to come home after my issues in the city. Dad had been the local handyman, and I was lucky enough to learn most of what he did for the town. Now that I'm back, it's my job, along with whatever other odd work anyone has for me. Most days, I bounce from place to place around town, painting, building, roofing, basically doing whatever needs to be done. I've never shied away from hard work, and I'm good at what I do. I'm still working on my degree; I just have to squeeze online classes and homework in between and after jobs. I can't give up my dream just because of a small setback.

And that's exactly what Chad was. A small setback. Granted, one that nearly ruined my life, but still. I'm home and safe now. It doesn't matter that I flinch sometimes when men get too close. I've managed to hide that as much as possible. No one here knows what happened, and I want to keep it that way.

I grab my truck keys and tool bag, not bothering to lock the door on my way out. I only lock it at night because Mama and Daddy insist. "A young woman living alone should keep her doors locked at night. Especially after what that monster did." Yes, ma'am. I never argued, and never will. But if I'm not here, there's no reason to lock it. If someone wanted my stuff, they'd just break in and take it anyway.

It's been a little slow this week with handyman work, but I'm keeping busy. My first stop is Katie's house. Her sink has been dripping, and Earl just got the parts in for me to fix it. I listen to her account of her most recent date while I work, splitting my attention so I don't miss anything.

She's been seeing Pete, Earl's son, for a month or so. "I like him, Court, but I'm just not sure he feels the same. It's like he's always distracted. He didn't even kiss me goodnight when he dropped me off!"

"What? That's crazy. Katie, he must have something going on at work or with his dad. You need to give him time. I know he's nuts about you. Okay? Don't worry, I'm sure your next date will be much better," I tell her, making a mental note to pass this little bit on to Ms. Gertrude so she can play matchmaker. I don't indulge in spreading gossip usually, but I know that Pete is as crazy about Katie as she is about him. I'm just not the person to handle the situation.

After finishing up at Katie's, Earl calls and I have to head to the hardware store. His network is giving him issues. I'm not finished with my classes yet, but I can definitely take a look and see what I can do. I'm excited to work on something computer related for a change. The entire town knows that I'm studying for an IT degree, and they're all pretty supportive.

That's not to say that I'm friends with everyone in town, because I'm not. There are some people here that I can't stand, and they seem to feel the same way about me. But they'd never do anything to hurt me, other than talking behind my back. And I don't care much about that.

"Mornin' Earl. What can I help ya with?" I ask as I walk into the hardware store.

"It's this confounded internet stuff again, Court. I just can't get it to connect. And of course, the new cash register doesn't work without it. I don't know why I let Petey talk me into that thing." Ah, there's Pete's distraction. His dad's been on his case about upgrading the registers.

"Well, Earl, I'll get this squared away in just a few minutes. Then you'll be up and running. Let's start by getting your cash drawer out so you can do business the old-fashioned way, shall we?" I text Pete and ask about popping the drawer and he responds with which buttons to push. Once that's open, Earl relaxes. I guess he thought the register would keep his money. A few minutes later, I have him back online and promise to check back tomorrow to make sure everything is running smoothly.

I stop off at the diner for lunch, and the gossip mill is in full force. Ms. Gertrude keeps trying to set me up with her grandson, Jake, even though he's dating some girl from the next town over. I don't let it get to me, though. I just smile at her and nod when she says she'll get him to call me. She means well, as do most of them.

These sweet little old ladies in my town are only trying to help me. You see, an unclaimed omega could get herself into serious trouble, especially if she has to go through her heat alone. Lucky for me, I'm a late bloomer. Most omegas start having heats when they turn twenty, but for whatever reason, I'm nine years past that, and have never had one. I've been to several doctors, all of which claim that everything checks out. There's nothing wrong with me. My body just isn't ready to create life yet. And I'm fine with that. I'm starting to wonder if I'm even an omega at all. Besides that, I don't have a mate or mates.

It's not that there aren't plenty of choices here in Miller Falls. There are, really. I'm just not attracted to any of them. And with New York fresh in my mind, I'm not ready for dating. My parents tried to send me away for school in the hopes that I'd find a pack and live happily ever after, but it didn't happen. I studied computer science and learned how to build computers and maintain networks, but I never found love. I have no idea if that's because of what happened with Chad, or if I just didn't try hard enough.

While I was away, my parents retired and took off to Florida. With my blessing, mind you. I fully supported the plan. Mama's arthritis had gotten so bad that she could barely move. She needed to be where it was warm. Our almost daily calls tell me that she's doing a lot better down there, and I wouldn't have it any other way.

So, that's how we got here. And now, I'm sitting at the diner, listening to the gossip while eating lunch and figuring out where else I need to go today. There's talk of new people moving in today. I miss part of the conversation, so I'm not sure where. I'll find out soon enough. This town is too small for secrets.

Over pie, I hear something that makes me shake my head. Poor Pete. His date with Katie didn't go well last night. She told her sister that she may not see him again. Of course, Ms. Gertrude steps right in and tells him to "get that girl some flowers" because that will fix the whole thing right up. She may be onto something there. Of all the residents of our small town, she's been married the longest. Her husband, Jack, is adorable when he brings flowers into the diner to surprise her. They were high school sweethearts and are still going strong today.

"Now, Courtney, sweetheart, you're going to let me get Jakey to call you this time, right?" she offers as she refills my coffee. I nod and smile. I won't argue with her, because it won't do any good.

"Yes, ma'am, Ms. Gertrude. And you're gonna tell me if you need anything from the store on my way home, right?" She nods her agreement as I twist the lid on my to-go cup. I take my coffee with me, stopping to pay my check at the counter.

I'm walking out the door when I hear Ms. Gertrude telling Annabelle, "We've got to do something for that girl. She needs a pack before her heat hits. It won't be long now." How does she know when I'll have my first heat? If the doctors can't tell me, and I have no idea, I wonder if the old lady knows something we don't.

I put the conversation out of my mind as I drive my dad's beat up work truck to my next job. I'll have to stay focused for this one. I can't be on a ladder at the Smith's painting their trim if I'm not focused. I park in front of the house and take a minute to breathe. I know Mrs. Smith will just be getting off the phone with Ms. Gertrude, and Mr. Smith will want to tell me exactly how to set up. I'll have to take both with a smile or risk losing their business. And I can't afford that right now. I'm barely making enough to cover the bills as it is.

A few hours later, I'm finished with the painting and on my way home. I should stop for dinner, but I'm exhausted. Today was a longer day than I had expected. I decide to go home and shower, then figure out dinner. Worst case, I'll have a frozen pizza.

I pull up to the house and my jaw drops. A moving truck sits next door at the old Johnson place. Hmm, that's curious. Mama didn't tell me they'd sold that house. And neither did anyone else for that matter. Now I'm suspicious that they're all gonna try to set me up with whoever is moving in.

I'll have to bake some cookies and make a welcome basket tonight to deliver in the morning. Mama would be pissed if I didn't welcome the new neighbors properly. I grab my keys and tool bag and head inside. I don't bother locking the truck, because if someone wanted it, they'd just knock and ask for the keys anyway.

I drop the tool bag inside the door and kick off my boots. I need a shower, but I want food more than that, so I head straight to the kitchen. After washing my hands, I pre-heat the oven and get the pizza ready to go in. Then I start gathering ingredients for Mama's blue-ribbon chocolate chip cookies. Or maybe I should bake some muffins? I don't know which the new neighbors would prefer.

Judging from the size of that moving truck, it's at least three or four people. Why not just make both? I nod to myself,

"Both. Always both." I turn on my speaker in the kitchen and pull up my favorite play list on my phone. Once I have all the ingredients spread out on my island, I start mixing up batter for fresh blueberry muffins and the chocolate chip cookies. I get both mixed and ready to go by the time the pizza is done. I put the muffins in first, standing at the island to eat while they cook. I clean up while the cookies are in the oven.

With that project complete, I head to the spare bedroom to find a basket. Mama left a bunch of them in the closet. *You never know when you'll need to show some hospitality.* I roll my eyes at her words playing in my head, then decide that she's got a point. I grab a basket that's big enough to hold the muffins and cookies, then head to the hall closet for a hand towel and oven mitt. I have to make it pretty, after all. Who knew that Mama's gift basket hobby would come in so handy? At least I didn't have to go buy anything.

Taking my time, I set up the basket and fill it with the goodies. Once I'm satisfied that it's exactly the way I want it, I grab one of the big bags Mama left under the sink and ease the basket into it. I decide to add a sunshine yellow ribbon to match the towel and mitt, then it's perfect. I'll pop over tomorrow before work and drop it off. Hopefully I'll get to meet the new neighbors and welcome them to town.

Now that I'm finished with the basket, exhaustion hits me. I lock the doors and head up to shower and sleep.

Two

Howdy, Neighbors!

COURTNEY

I WAKE EARLIER THAN usual after a fitful night of sleep. There's no reason to even try and go back to sleep. I might as well get up and get ready for my day. Being up and about early will give me time to meet the neighbors anyway. I carefully pick out casual clothes, knowing that I'll be painting today, I opt for a comfy pair of cotton bibbed overalls and a tank top. I run a brush through my golden strands, satisfied that at least my hair has decided to cooperate today.

Then, even though it's ridiculous, I put on a little make up. First impressions and all, you know. I take my tool bag and the basket out to the truck, slipping my keys in my pocket. After dropping off the tools, I take a deep breath and walk over to the neighbors' house. I knock on the door and wait.

Shit, what if they don't get up as early? Fuck, I should have waited until I knew they were up and not busy. But how would I know that? Damn it, Court, stop. I'm sure they're decent people and they're not gonna be mad if you woke them up.

It's been a minute, so I raise my hand to knock again when the door opens to a shirtless man wearing thin black pajama bottoms. I can't help but lick my lips at the sight. He clears his throat and I know that I've been caught staring. "Uh, sorry. I'm your neighbor and made you some goodies as a welcome basket."

A hesitant smile plays across his lips. Then I notice his eyes, warm brown pools that I could get lost in. His sandy brown hair is cut short, and he's trying hard to scowl at me. Ah, the grumpy one. This should be fun.

Before he responds, another man bounces up behind him, wrapping his arms around the first man possessively. Oh. The second man is a little shorter than the first, with chestnut brown hair and the greenest eyes I've ever seen. Damn, Court, don't start drooling. It's obvious that they're together.

"Hi! I'm Nick, please ignore Colin. He's cranky before coffee. Which is ready by the way. Please come in. Thank you so much for the gift." At Nick's insistence, Colin turns and walks away. Nick takes the basket and gestures for me to follow him. I know that I should refuse the offer, but he's just so cute that I find myself following him into the kitchen.

Just when I think this yum sandwich can't get any better, I see hunk number three, sitting at the table, reading something on a tablet. Nick heads up introductions. "Kent, this is…Wait, I didn't get your name."

"Courtney. Courtney Harris. I live next door. I made some muffins and cookies to welcome you to the neighborhood." Why is it so hard to form coherent sentences around these three?

"Kent Olsen. A pleasure to meet you." He stands and extends a hand to shake. When I put my hand in his, he brings it to his lips and presses a sweet kiss on the back of my hand. My stomach flutters. Maybe there's a chance after all. Wait, what am I thinking? I can't just jump into bed with the new guy because he kisses my hand.

"We've kind of met already, but I'm Nick Bailey. And the crabby pants with his coffee over there is Colin Price." Nick nods at Colin, who grunts. Does he not like me, or is it just too early for him? I'd love to find out.

"I'm really sorry to interrupt your morning," I say, noticing that none of them are fully dressed. Nick is in a pair of green basketball shorts. Kent is wearing a dark blue pair of jeans that look like they were painted on him. All three men display their chiseled chests proudly. And from their scents, I can tell that Kent and Nick are alphas, while Colin is a beta. The smell of caramel, chocolate, and cherries fills the air. I can't tell which scent is which, they're so permeated in this room. But they smell delicious.

Maybe his designation is why Colin is so cranky. "Don't worry about it. We were just debating where to get breakfast.

It seems you've solved that issue. Please, sit and join us. Would you like coffee or juice?" Kent asks, tearing into the basket and pulling out the muffins.

For whatever reason, I can't refuse his offer. I don't know if I'm mesmerized by so much chest on display, or if it's those baby blue eyes that entice me to stay. It could even be the way his jeans cup his ass. I'm not sure, and right now, I don't care. I sit in the chair Nick has pulled out for me. "Coffee would be great, with a little sugar and cream if you have it."

Nick takes the seat next to me, clearly not wanting to let someone else have it. I'm getting so many mixed signals here that I'm not sure if I'm coming or going. Colin takes the seat on the other side of Nick, as far away from me as possible. Maybe he just takes a bit to warm up to people.

Kent serves the coffee, just the way I like it, and the muffins. I'm nervous to see if they like them, and this feels more like a date than meeting new neighbors. But it's obvious that these three are together. Unless—nah, Court, let it go. They could be a pack looking for an omega, but you are not going to offer. Not right after meeting them.

"Thank you," I say. I can feel the heat of my blush tinging my cheeks.

"You're welcome. And thank you for bringing us breakfast." Kent sits in the seat next to me, purposefully scooting it closer to me. Colin scowls harder. Interesting. So many mixed signals.

"So, what do you guys do? If you don't mind me asking. I'm sorry if that sounds nosey. You don't have to tell me," I'm rambling and I can't seem to stop.

"It's fine. We don't mind questions," Nick responds. "You are having breakfast with the founders of OBP Tech."

My eyes open wide. There's no way. These guys are my idols. They're the reason I started studying computers and tech. My dream was to get a job at their company. How funny is this day?

"What? No way! I've been following you guys since you opened. You've got some really impressive stuff in the works." And just like that I'm relaxed and engaged in this conversation.

Kent, Nick, and I talk a bit about what the company is working on, and my studies. "What do you do here?" Kent asks. My cheeks turn pink and suddenly I'm embarrassed to tell them I'm a handyman.

"Well, my parents recently retired to Florida, so I've taken over my father's business. I am Harris Contracting. So, I do a little bit of everything." I expect them to laugh, and Colin does not disappoint. I don't think I like him.

"Colin, that's rude," Nick admonishes him.

"It's okay, really. I understand. My job is nothing like yours. And he's allowed to have his opinion." Why am I defending him? It was rude, and he gives me a knowing look.

Kent glares at Colin. "It's not okay, and he knows it. Apologize. Now." And just like that, I know which one is head alpha, and I've made an enemy. Colin glares back at him, then turns to me.

He pastes on a fake smile. "I'm so sorry to have offended you, princess." Then he turns back to Kent. "Happy now?" He slides his chair back forcefully and storms out of the room.

"I'm sorry. I would say he's not usually like that, but that's pretty much Colin. Please don't hold his behavior against us. We'd really like to be friends." Kent's apology nearly makes me cry. Why do his words have so much impact on me.

"Really, it's okay. Not everyone is gonna like you. I'm okay with it. But yeah, I'd like for us to be friends." Am I flirting with him?

"He's been bitchy since we moved. He wanted to stay in LA. But it makes more sense to set up the new branches of the business ourselves. Then there's the stalker," Nick starts to explain, but Kent gives him a look. "Sorry."

"You guys have a stalker? That's crazy." I know that I shouldn't ask, but I can't stop myself.

"The issue is being handled," Kent replies. "Nick gets a little excited about things sometimes. Don't let it worry you."

He easily steers the conversation away from the stalker and Colin. We discuss their business more and he asks questions about my studies. I know that I could learn so much from these guys, and I hope I get the chance.

NICK

I know the moment I mention our stalker that I've fucked up. Kent didn't want people to know we were hiding out. I tried to explain that moving here wouldn't stop Terri from finding us. Especially if those letters she wrote were any indication of what she wanted to do. I'm also not sure why I felt like I needed to tell Courtney about it right now.

There's just something about her that makes me want to tell her everything. I want her to know us and to accept us.

She's gorgeous. I wonder if she knows that. I want to pull her into my arms and show her, but that's not something I would do without Kent and Colin being on board. From her scent, I can tell she's an omega. Strawberries. Mmm, it makes me want to dive in and taste her. I shake the thought away as Kent asks her about her classes.

How long should I wait to ask her out? I mean. No, Nick, you can't do that. Even if Kent likes her too, it has to be a group decision. I can't just go around making pack decisions without input from the other guys, especially since Kent is our head alpha. I shouldn't have to keep reminding myself of that, but I do.

I wonder if I can talk him into hiring her. If she looks this good in overalls, imagine if she was wearing a tight little pencil skirt with a button up blouse. I can't stop my cock from reacting to that thought. I guess that means I'll be sitting here for a bit longer than I had planned. I don't mind, as long as I get to be near our new friend.

I imagine what it will be like, pressing my lips to hers, laying claim to what's mine. No, I can't think like that. I'm gonna have to talk to Kent and Colin about this. I've just met this girl, and now I want to claim her? Something about her has my alpha nature on edge.

"Well, if you need any help navigating the town or its inhabitants, just let me know. I've only been back in town for a few weeks, but I grew up here. I know everyone here. If you need anything, just let me know. If I can't fix it, I'm sure I'll know who can."

Wait, it sounds like she's leaving. I got lost in my thoughts and missed half the conversation. My heart races. I have to find a way to get her to stay. "You're not running off so soon, are you?" I know the question sounds desperate, and I hope I don't scare her off.

"I have to get to work. But I'm sure we'll see each other around. We are neighbors, after all," she says with a wink. Does that mean she's interested? I mean, I feel like she was flirting with us, but Colin put a damper on everything this morning and I'm not sure.

"How about a tour of the new building once we get it set up?" The offer is out my mouth before I realize that I should have asked Kent first. Fuck, I hope this doesn't piss him off. If it does, I'll deal with it.

"That sounds great. Just let me know when. Here's my number if you need anything. Just call or text. I'll see you guys later." Kent walks her to the door, which is a relief, because my dick is still standing at attention, and these shorts would do nothing to hide that.

As soon as she leaves, I melt into my chair. Damn that omega is hot. When he comes back into the room, Kent laughs. "What?" I ask, even though I know what he's going to say.

"Someone has a crush on our new neighbor," he teases.

"I can't help it. Did you see her?" I wipe the imaginary drool off my chin and he laughs again. I walk across the room and pull him into my arms. He's taller than me, and I look up at him. "Besides, I think you like her too."

Kent leans down and catches my lips with his, wrapping his arms around me. He whispers against my lips, "So what if I do?" I run my tongue along his lips, making him kiss me again. My hands tangle in his hair, pulling it free from the top knot he keeps it in. His hands slide down and grip my ass. At this moment, I don't mind letting him take control.

"I wonder what Colin's problem is," I say when we part from our embrace.

"You know he's still upset about Terri being crazy," Kent responds. I know that, but I want him to like this girl.

"Do you think he'll warm up to her?"

"I know you're hoping that she'll be the one, but you have to be willing to take things slow this time. Don't push her, or Colin. They have to accept it on their own terms. Understood?" I hate when he talks to me like he's my dad instead of my lover.

I roll my eyes at him. "Yes, Dad." He swats my ass as he walks away.

"Keep being a brat, and you'll get punished," he warns. I'm not worried. I like his punishments. But I can't focus on that right now, or I won't get anything done today. I already know that I'm going to be craving strawberries all day. I make a mental note to pick some up from the grocery store this afternoon. Maybe I'll pick up a thank you gift for our new neighbor to show our appreciation for her hospitality. I'm also going to make a mental note of every reason to see her again.

I head upstairs to shower and start working on a plan for just how I'm going to convince everyone of what I already know. That Courtney should be our omega.

Three

How About Dinner?

COURTNEY

I KEEP AN EYE on the new neighbors for the next few days. I know that I should forget about this attraction, but every time I close my eyes, I see one of them standing in front of me, shirtless and with lust-filled eyes looking back at me. My daydreams are starting to interfere with my work.

I smash my thumb with a hammer at the Smith's and they insist I take the rest of the day off. I'm disappointed because I need the money. But I'm relieved because it means I can go home and stare at the guys next door. I'm hopeless. They didn't really express any interest in me beyond being friends.

Within a few days, I've managed to convince myself that everything I thought I saw was all in my imagination. I can't help but notice that every night this week, they've had take out delivered. It's not my business, but I know how few places there are to order from around here.

I check the fridge to see what I have and make a decision. I jot a few things down that I need from the store before I head next door. There's no reason for this to be awkward, Court. Just invite them to dinner. The worst they can do is say no. It's not a big deal. You're not looking for mates anyway.

I knock on the door, and it opens immediately. "Oh, hi, Nick. I barely even knocked. Were you watching me from the window?" I joke. The flush of his cheeks tells me that he may have been doing just that. Oh, shit. Maybe he is interested. Or maybe he's just like Ms. Gertrude and just wants to know what his neighbors are up to. Let. It. Go.

"I, uh, I. Movement caught my attention. I was coming to see who was walking by. Sorry, I know that sounds creepy," he blurts. I want to hug him for being as awkward as I am. But that would be too forward of me.

"I just stopped by to invite you guys to dinner tonight. If you don't have plans. And if you want to. I'm making spaghetti with meat sauce and garlic toast." Did I really just say meat sauce? Kill me now. Why am I making this so weird?

"Oh, that sounds great. Come on in. I'll just get Colin and Kent and make sure that neither of them has anything planned." He opens the door wider and escorts me to the living room. "I'll be right back. Feel free to look around."

I'm shocked at how beautiful this room is. They've decorated it perfectly. It suits each of their personalities. The floor to ceiling book case is fully stocked with everything from the classics to modern romance. Hmm, Rose Wulf and N.A. Jameson. Nice taste, boys. All they're missing is some Kaytie Marie, but I could hook them up with that.

Once I finish perusing the book case, I check out the photos on the mantle. It looks like these three have been pretty much inseparable since they were kids. That's a beautiful bond. I wish I had more of those. Katie and I are close, but not like that. I'm still staring at their memories when someone clears his throat. I jump and spin around to find Colin standing closer than I would expect.

"See something interesting, princess?" Why is this man so hateful?

"Maybe. Do you?" I lick my lips, watching him watch me. I can tell that he's curious, but he's holding back. I wonder why. Tentatively, I take a step forward, stopping an inch away from touching him. He doesn't move. "I feel like you do, but you don't want anyone to know that. Am I right?" I keep my voice low so that the other two don't hear what I say, since I see them entering the room at that moment.

I've backed him into a corner and I have no idea how he'll respond. He doesn't seem to notice the other two and continues staring at me. I can feel the heat building between us. Part of me wants to slug him, and the rest wants to climb him like a tree. I know if I move right now, I'll be letting him know he's won. So, I don't.

My breath comes in quiet pants, with my heartbeat escalating. I'm sure he can see the effect he's having on me. He seems more concerned with his own reaction to my closeness. I'm not sure what I expect to happen here. After a moment of staring at each other like this, he leans closer. His lips are a whisper away from mine. "You'll never know."

My eyes flutter closed with his words. When I open them, he's gone. What the fuck just happened? I struggle to get my breathing under control. I can feel the panic attack coming on, and I'm not surprised by it. An angry man being that close to me, with sexual tension crackling between us would be enough to set me off any day.

Before I collapse, Kent's arms wrap around me and he pulls me to his chest. "It's okay, sweetheart. Just breathe. I'm not sure what just happened, but it looked intense. Just take a minute and breathe. I've got you." I bury my face in his chest and breathe in his caramel scent. It calms me a bit, but my breaths are still ragged and I'm worried I'll pass out. "Nick, grab her a bottle of water."

Kent eases me to the couch and sits down, pulling me onto his lap. I know it's not normal, but I can't think about that right now. This just feels right. "You don't have to tell me, sweetheart, but if you want to talk about it, Nick and I are here."

I shake my head. I just met these guys. I can't drop my trauma on them right now. I take the offered bottle of water and drink deeply, sitting up a little. "I just wanted to invite you to dinner. I don't know what happened with Colin, but it freaked me out. I'm sorry for reacting that way." As I speak, Kent is rubbing slow circles on my back, with his other arm draped around my waist.

I know that I should get up and leave, but I can't force myself to move right now. Nick's chocolate scent mixes with Kent's and I know that I'm done for. I want these men more than I will ever admit. But I'm also terrified of that desire.

"Dinner sounds lovely. Where would you like to go?" Kent asks, still rubbing my back.

"She said she wanted to cook for us," Nick offers. I nod, unable to speak. I take a couple of deep breaths, calming myself more.

"I want to make spaghetti."

"We'd love to join you for dinner. Spaghetti is my favorite," Kent replies.

KENT

I can tell Courtney is starting to calm down and relax. I want to know what set her off so I can hurt the person responsible. From her reaction, I know it wasn't really Colin, but more what he represented in that moment. I enjoy holding her as long as I can, knowing that Nick is staring at us. He'll wait until she leaves to say 'I told you so' but that won't make it any less true. I like her. I was immediately attracted to her, and I'm sure Colin was too. He's just still too raw over Terri to handle those feelings.

"Nick, why don't you check on Colin? He seemed a bit upset. I think Courtney is okay now," I say, triggering her to climb off my lap. I don't want to let her go, but I can't keep her there against her will.

"Okay," he says cheerfully. Before he walks away, he pulls Courtney into his arms and hugs her. "I'll see you in a little while, honey." I hope I can get Colin on board, so Nick doesn't get destroyed when this falls apart. He's not one for casual hook ups, and he's already attached to the new neighbor. That's not to say that I'm not, but it's worse for him.

After he leaves, I can tell that she feels awkward about what just happened because she's wringing her hands. "Come here." I hold out my hand and she walks into my arms easily. "I understand that a panic attack can be a source of embarrassment, but I hope that you know you're among friends here. We would never judge you for that."

I look down at her, and she tilts her head up. Our lips are close enough to touch. All I need to do is move less than an inch. Her breath on my lips urges me to close the distance. But I can't. I won't make a move on her right after she had an attack because of another man. It wouldn't be right.

COLIN

I storm away after my confrontation with Courtney. I can't take being near her for one more moment. Fuck, she's gorgeous. But I can't go there. Not after Terri. I can't put my mates through that again. And since Courtney is even prettier than Terri, that means she has double the potential for crazy. I know I shouldn't have spoken to her the way I did. I had to turn and leave to keep from pulling her into my arms and kissing her. What the fuck is wrong with me?

When Nick finds me a little while later, I'm in my room playing Diablo to blow off some steam. I know he's there before he taps on the doorframe. "Come on in. You know you don't have to knock."

He quietly crosses the room and drops to his knees next to my chair. "Are you okay, love?" I glance at him because there's something in his voice. Does he feel rejected because of how I've acted? I pause the game and move my chair back, pulling him onto my lap.

I press my lips to his, coaxing him to let me in. I like that Nick lets me take control when I need it. Somehow this sweet alpha knows exactly what I need and gives it to me. It helps that he likes to be dominated sometimes. We hold each other, kissing lazily as if we have nothing else to do. I can't admit to him, or to Kent, that I'm scared of losing them over Courtney. I love them so much, but I'm not ready for an omega.

Nick pulls away first. "Seriously, are you okay? You were pretty harsh with Court, and she had a panic attack after you left. She's okay now, but it reminded me of the way you react to talk of she who shall not be named."

I laugh at Nick's reference to Terri. And he's right, I noticed that Courtney was starting to freeze like I did when I realized what I'd done to my family. I'd put them at risk, and there was no excuse for that. "I'm okay. Really. I just couldn't be that close to her anymore. I don't even know what came over me. I'm sorry I was rude again." I hang my head, because there's nothing else I can do.

Nick tilts my head up with one finger and gently kisses me again. "Colin, we love you. You know that. But you have to talk to us. We can't help if we don't understand the problem."

"I don't know. I feel guilty about everything that forced us to move here. And being around her sets me off. I'm just not ready for anything like that again. Not yet."

"Oh, love. We're not going to push you into anything you don't want. We don't even know if she's interested that way. She just came to invite us to dinner."

COURTNEY

With Kent's lips so close, I can't resist lifting onto my toes and pressing mine against them. He melts into the kiss easily, and for just a moment, everything else falls away. His arms hold me tighter, as if he's afraid I'll run away. I snake my hands up into his hair, pulling it free of that top knot he's always wearing. I use that leverage to deepen the kiss, my tongue stroking against his. Then I realize exactly what I've done and jump away from him.

"I'm so sorry. That was completely inappropriate. I don't know what to say. I understand if you don't want to come to dinner," I ramble, because I'm upset and nervous.

"Sweetheart, take a breath. You didn't do anything wrong. It's okay. Yes, things are complicated, for everyone involved here. But we'll be there for dinner, unless you've changed your mind?" This man. How does he always seem to know exactly what to say? And he's being so kind, after I all but assaulted him in his own home.

"Please come to dinner. It'll be ready at six, but you guys are welcome to come over a little early if you'd like. I have to run to the store now. Thank you so much for everything you did for me today. I'll see you later?" I can't stick around. I don't want to be here when he tells the other two what I did. And I'm sure he'll tell them.

I rush out of the house before he can stop me. Once I'm in my truck, I take a couple of deep breaths. What was it about Colin that set me off? Probably his anger. He's so angry. But it didn't seem like that was directed at me. I close my eyes for a minute, letting myself remember the feel of Kent's lips against mine. Fuck, that kiss was hot. I should go back inside and change my panties, but I don't want to.

I know that I have to get some work done today, even if it's just for my classes. Since my slight injury, I can't do anything outside of the house. I glance down at my thumb and wince. It's black and blue, but I don't feel the pain anymore. I'll wear the bruises as a reminder that I need to be focused on what I'm doing, not daydreaming about three sexy men who live next door.

Three? Am I fantasizing about Colin too? Hmm, I guess I am. I already knew I was attracted to dark and broody, so it doesn't surprise me. I pull out of the drive and head to the store. I need to get groceries, and walking around Cooper's might calm my racing heart down.

Or maybe I should go see Ms. Gertrude at the diner for a shake. No, I can't do that. She'll know that something is up. Somehow that woman seems to be able to read my mind. Nope, Cooper's it is, then.

NICK

I LET COLIN TAKE control of our interaction. I can tell when he needs that power. Being a beta, he's always been denied that. I hate how society treats betas, and omegas, for that matter. Neither one is below an alpha. I'm just more outgoing than they are, so I get more respect. It's ridiculous really.

My heart hurts for Colin. I want to make him feel better. Kent walks into the room a little while after I did. "Did she leave?" I ask, not moving from where I sit on Colin. He nods and walks over to us, leaning down to kiss me, then Colin.

"She did. And that panic attack had an interesting effect on her. I love and respect you two, so I'm not hiding anything. She kissed me, and I thoroughly enjoyed it." When Colin makes a face, Kent holds up a hand. "That doesn't mean anything else is going to happen. She thinks that she's crossed some boundary and apologized profusely. But from that kiss, I can tell that she's interested. We have to decide if we are."

"It's too soon," Colin says quietly.

"I know, but chances like this don't happen every day. I can tell you, Colin, she's not Terri. There's no risk of us going through what we did before." Kent's easy dismissal of Colin's argument tells me that he's already decided. Courtney will be our omega.

I can barely contain my excitement. "You know that you don't have to rush things with her, Col. It's okay to take things slow. We can court her. Ha! We can court Court. That's funny." I laugh at my own joke, while the other two groan. I'm a sucker for dad jokes.

"Okay, okay. I have to admit, I'm attracted to her. That's part of the problem. I can't get what happened with Terri out of my head. And it's messing with me when I'm around Courtney. But if both of you are into her, I can give things a try. We have to take it slow, and you have to understand that I'm not going to be as easily affectionate with her as you two are."

Colin's words sting. "Do you want us to not be affectionate with her?" I hope that he doesn't say yes. I'm dying to touch her again. That hug felt so good, and I'm a little jealous of Kent kissing her.

He hugs me tighter. "That's not what I'm saying at all. You two always have the freedom to do what you want. I don't control that. Just don't expect me to be so freely affectionate with someone I don't really know."

Fuck me. We're going to date Courtney. Well, as long as she's interested. I wonder if Kent will bring it up at dinner. Maybe it's too soon, especially with her panic attack earlier. I guess I'll just let our head alpha take control and go with the flow.

COURTNEY

After the grocery store, I drive around town for a bit to relax myself. I shouldn't have kissed Kent. I know it, but I can't feel bad about it. It was the best kiss of my life. I need to push that thought down and forget about it. The three of them are obviously together, from the way they easily show affection to each other. I want desperately to be part of that. But I won't push my way in.

If they're interested, they'll say something. I pull into the drive and take a minute to gather my thoughts. A glance next door has me drooling again. Colin is mowing the yard. If only he didn't hate me, we could have something amazing. I would love to explore all those muscles. With my tongue.

Fuck. No, Court. You cannot lick the neighbor. It's impolite. I grab my groceries and head into the house without another look. I carefully put everything away, then decide that a shower is in order. Just as I'm heading up the stairs, someone knocks on the door. Okay, this is odd. I turn and walk to the front door, opening it without even looking to see who's here.

Suddenly I'm face to face with a sweaty, shirtless grump of a man. "Oh, Colin. Please come in. I'll get you some water." I head into the kitchen without waiting to see if he's following. Even if he stays on the porch, I can bring him a bottle of water. I grab one from the fridge and turn around, almost bumping into him. His closeness starts to set me off again.

My breath comes in pants and my heart races. Why does he get to me this way? "Thanks," he says, taking the bottle from me and draining it without moving from my personal space. I can't back away, because he has me pinned between him and the fridge.

"What, um, what can I do for you?" I squeak out, barely able to talk. I can feel my knees shake and I know I'm on the verge of a full-on panic attack. I lift my eyes to meet his, and can see that I'm having a similar effect on him.

He takes a careful step back and we both breathe a little easier. "I'm having a problem with the trimmer. Since you're the town's handyman, maybe you can take a look?"

"Oh, sure. Let me grab my tools." I use the space he gave me to dart around him and head for my tool bag at the front door.

"Courtney?" he calls quietly. I freeze. "I'm sorry about before. It's not you. I have some—issues, that I'm working on." Wow, an apology from the grump. It's not a profession of undying love, but it's a start.

I turn around to face him. "Start over? Hi, I'm Courtney, your neighbor. I'd love to be friends."

He takes my outstretched hand, but doesn't shake it. Instead, he holds it gingerly. "Colin. And I'd like that, princess."

COLIN

I know that I should let Nick or Kent handle asking her to fix the trimmer. It's the smarter move. But since they're checking out office spaces today, I have no choice. It's amusing because the reason they left me at home was because I needed a break from people. And here I am reaching out to one. At least it gives me a chance to apologize.

The moment my hand touches hers, I know that I'm going to lose my heart to this omega. I say a silent prayer that I'm not wrong about this one. Terri was a mistake I will not make again.

Courtney grabs her tool bag, flinching a little when I take it from her. "I'll get it." I smile at her, and I'm certain she's absolutely confused. Me too, girl, me too. She follows me over to the house and into the back yard where the offensive piece of machinery is laying in the yard. It was all I could do to not throw it.

I set the tool bag down. "Well, here it is. What do you need me to do?"

"Just step back and watch. I'll get it going in no time." Her confidence amazes me. I watch intently as she checks the gas and line, then tries to start it. When it doesn't work, she starts fiddling with parts of the engine that I wouldn't mess with. That's when I notice that her thumb is black and blue.

"What happened to your thumb? Are you okay?" I can't stop myself from asking, even though I'm not sure how she's going to react.

"Oh. I got distracted and smashed it with a hammer. It's okay," she says as she works.

"It doesn't look okay. It looks like it might be broken," I insist. "You should get it x-rayed."

She laughs. "I probably should, but I won't. I can't afford for it to be broken. I have to work. It's bad enough that I had to take today off because I did it. The Smiths insisted that I take the day off. That was nice of them, but it won't get my bills paid." She looks annoyed that she shared that with me, but I'm glad she did. It gives me ideas.

"Why are you the town handyman? You're going to school for IT. Couldn't you get something more fitting for work?"

"Not around here. Unless you guys are hiring? Because yours is the only tech company in the area, in case you haven't noticed." She laughs as I contemplate her words. "I was kidding about the job, though. I don't expect you guys to hire me."

I nod in understanding. Still, it's not a bad idea. She knows this area, and everyone in the town. Having her work with us could be quite useful. I'll have to talk to Kent and Nick about it before dinner. Or after. We'll see how it goes.

The trimmer roars to life and my jaw drops. "All fixed," she says standing and wiping her hands on her jeans.

KENT

Looking at properties with Nick is relaxing. He gets along with everyone, and is having an animated conversation with the realtor about exactly what we're looking for in a building. It gives me a chance to watch him, and check out details of each property without feeling pressured. I love watching how much of a people person he is. I've been trying to figure out how he does it for years. It's one of the reasons I fell in love with him.

But today I'm a little distracted because Colin seems to be in a weird place. He needed a break from people, which is fine. I'm just worried about trying to add Courtney to our mix. The three of us get along really well already, and I don't want to mess that up.

Sharon must have asked me a question while I was lost in thought. It takes me a minute to realize that she and Nick are staring at me. "I'm sorry, I got distracted."

"No problem. I just asked how you like this one. Nick seems to think it would be perfect for what you need," she offers without judgment.

"Oh. I'm just not sure. Can we do another walkthrough? I promise to stay focused this time." I have got to get my shit together or this deal will fall through. There aren't any other realtors in Miller Falls, and we need to buy a property soon.

"Of course, whatever you need." I like that she's amenable, but I feel guilty for wasting her time. I should have pushed everything away earlier and paid attention the first time.

We go over the floorplan, with Nick adding in where he sees certain things fitting. Sharon tells us a little more about the history of the town and this building in particular. By the time they're done showing me the building again, I completely agree with Nick. This one is perfect.

"Sharon, I think we'd like to make an offer for this one. Can we discuss the price at your office, or would you prefer to do that here?" I don't want to wait, even though I should get Colin's opinion too.

"I have the paperwork with me, unless you'd rather be in my office to decide on your offer," she responds, pulling out paperwork and setting it on a counter top.

"This will work perfectly. Could we take a look at the asking price and property details?"

She hands me the paperwork, already prepared for my question. "I'll give you two a moment to discuss without feeling like I'm hovering." Sharon walks outside and around the side of the building. No doubt, she'll be having a smoke while we talk.

"What do you think about that asking price?" Nick looks at me expectantly.

"I think it's too low for what the property is worth."

COURTNEY

Colin and I stand there, staring at each other for a moment longer than I would have expected. "Thank you," he offers, taking the trimmer from me. "How did you know what to do to make it work?"

"My dad taught me about small engines. He taught me everything about his job, really. And I'm not half bad at it if I do say so," I tease, bumping my shoulder to his arm. For a moment he tenses, and I worry that I've done something wrong.

"What do I owe you?" The question throws me off and I make a face.

"What do you mean?"

"For fixing the trimmer. What do I owe you?" he asks again.

"Oh, nothing. Neighbors help each other out here. Besides, we're friends, right?" I hope that he hasn't changed his mind about that.

"Then you'll have to let me help you with something so we're square," he insists. I pause for a moment, trying to think of something I could use help with.

"You can come over a little early tonight and help me make dinner if you want," I offer. He nods.

"I can do that. Let me finish the yard and shower, then I'll be over." My heart races, and I can smell my reaction to his response. Strawberry scent fills the air, and he takes a deep breath. I worry that he'll get upset, then I get a hint of cherry mixing with my pheromones. Damn, he smells good.

"I'll leave you to it," I say before practically running back to my house. What is it with these men that makes me act so stupid? I'm not looking for anything, and I don't want to force anyone into something they obviously don't want.

I glance over my shoulder and see him finishing his trimming. I'm relieved that he's not paying any attention to me now. I have to figure out what it is about him that reminds me so much of Chad so I can get past it. Otherwise, I'll never survive being his friend.

Once I'm back inside, I spend some time tidying up. My house isn't messy, but I don't clean nearly as much as I should. I pull out the vacuum and dust the living and dining rooms. I put my ear buds in when I'm ready to vacuum. I dance around the house cleaning, realizing that I'm in a way better mood than I have been in weeks.

I wonder if it'll be obvious to everyone that these men have piqued my interest. I don't want to admit it to myself, much less anyone else. After I finish the living and dining rooms, I move to the kitchen. I keep the dishes done, so all I need to do in here is sweep and mop. I do that quickly, then clean the guest bathroom and head upstairs to gather my laundry. If I'm cleaning, I might as well get everything done before I need to start prepping dinner.

Dinner and a Proposition

COURTNEY

With the house clean and everything set up for dinner prep, all I have to do is wait for Colin to get here. I don't really need help with dinner, but he seemed insistent that he would either help me with something or pay me. Just when I start to get bored, there's a knock on the door.

"Right on time. I was getting things ready," I tell Colin as I let him in. "Will Nick and Kent be over soon?" I don't know how safe it is for me to be alone with any of them after what happened earlier with Kent. He follows me to the kitchen, looking around as we walk.

"They're finishing up a contract with the realtor, then they'll be over. I spoke with them a bit ago," he explains.

"Okay. That means we're on our own for a bit. Are we going to be okay?" I'm still not sure how he feels about me, and I don't want to make him uncomfortable.

"I'm good if you are. Is it weird for me to be here alone?" He looks as nervous as I feel.

I shake my head. "No, we're adults. We can cook dinner together without supervision." I turn on the stove to heat the skillet. Colin grabs the stock pot and fills it with water, adding salt when he sets it back on the stove.

"Good. I'm glad that I don't make you too uncomfortable. I still feel bad about before. I am generally grumpier than Kent and Nick, but I'm not usually rude. I know you have no reason to believe me, though." We fall into a companionable silence as we prepare the veggies that I'll put into the sauce. I always start with the premade jar, then spruce it up with veggies and spices. I start breaking the ground beef into pieces as it cooks.

My hands brush his as I grab ingredients and I feel a tingle of anticipation. My heart is racing again, but not from fear. His scent gets to me in the best way, and goosebumps flash up my arms.

With the meat cooked, I start building the sauce around it. "Well, that's all we can do for now. The sauce needs to cook so the flavors can meld together." I turn and find him right behind me again. I step to my left, moving toward the island. Colin steps with me, caging me in.

"What's wrong, princess? You seem nervous," he smirks. I know that he can sense my reaction to him. I'm not sure how I feel about him being this close to me right now. We've started over and are supposed to be friends now. But this is a little closer than I usually stand to my friends.

He takes another step closer, and my back is pressed up against the island. "Are you scared of me?" he asks, genuine concern filling his voice. I shake my head. No, this isn't fear that I'm feeling. "Tell me." His insistence makes me take a deep breath so I can answer him.

"I'm not scared of you. Nervous, yes. But not scared." I look up at him and lick my lips. I want to taste him, but I can't make that move. Not after earlier. He acted like he hated me, now suddenly he wants me? It's too confusing.

"Let's see if we can calm those nerves, shall we?" I nod at his question and he lowers his mouth to mine, gently pressing a kiss to my lips. I gasp and he takes that opportunity to deepen the kiss, pulling me into his arms.

I relax against him, letting him take control and dominate the kiss. It's filled with passion and promise. I don't want it to end, but I know that it can't continue forever. When he pulls away, he looks at me for a minute, as if he's trying to put the pieces of a puzzle together. Then he nods and steps back.

"What was that about?" I ask breathlessly.

"I needed to see for myself what Kent was so worked up about. You're an excellent kisser, princess."

My cheeks heat at the compliment, and I wonder exactly what Kent said to him about our kiss. I knew that he would tell them, but I have no idea how he felt about it. "What do you mean, he was worked up?"

"In a good way. Don't worry. He had nothing but good things to say about your kiss and what it did to him."

"I'm still sorry about it. I shouldn't have thrown myself at him like that. It was disrespectful and I was raised better." I know it's an excuse, but I can't stop the words from coming out.

Colin grins at me. "He wanted you to kiss him. You should know that. And now Nick is going to flip out because he didn't get to be next." His laugh made my heart skip.

"So, is this like some kind of competition? I thought you guys were together."

"We are, but that doesn't stop us from appreciating a beautiful woman when we see one." His words make me blush again. I drop my eyes to the floor, raking them down his body as they go. I can see what kissing me did to him. Interesting. Maybe there's a chance for this to work after all.

Is that even what I want? Three weeks ago, I would have said no. But now, I don't know. These three stir feelings in me that I'm not ready to deal with. "Thank you," I whisper.

"Can I ask you something personal?"

My head jerks up and our eyes meet. "Okay." I'm scared of what he's going to ask, but I have to know.

"Why don't you have a pack already?" Oh, that. Well, it was bound to come up at some point.

"I almost did. Would it be okay if I save that story for dinner? That way I don't have to tell it more than once."

COLIN

I know that I shouldn't have asked about her lack of a pack, and I probably shouldn't have kissed her. But working next to her in the kitchen like this got me all worked up. Her strawberry scent lingers on me, and I had to know if she tasted as good as she smells.

I can't push her for the information, so I nod when she asks to talk about it at dinner. I help her set the table and finish cooking. Then when a knock comes at the door, I answer it. "Hey guys, it's about time you got here."

Nick and Kent look confused, but come in anyway. "I thought you were running late," Nick accuses. I smirk at him and motion for them to follow me. Kent has a bottle of Cabernet Sauvignon, so I motion to the kitchen where Courtney is tending to the pasta.

"We brought wine," he offers as he sets the bottle on the island.

"Oh, that's lovely. Thank you," she replies, grabbing the opener and passing it over to him. This is turning out to be a pretty comfortable dinner so far. I'm sure it will get a little awkward when she explains the answer to my question, but we'll be here to help her through it.

It's funny how our conversation earlier changed how I feel around her. And that kiss didn't hurt either. I can still taste her on my lips. I smile when Nick leans in for a kiss and realizes. "You didn't," he says.

With a smirk, I respond, "I did. And I helped make dinner."

He glares at me, and I'd be willing to bet that by the end of the day, Courtney will have kissed all three of us. It's not a competition, but I feel as if I've won just for having the experience. It makes me more comfortable about the idea of asking her to be our omega. But we need answers first. Those should come with dinner.

And I'm sure they'll also come with more questions. I'll have to explain about Terri and why I feel responsible for that situation. If she's still interested after that, we'll figure things out.

Kent gets the wine situated and I grab the huge serving bowl full of spaghetti and sauce from Courtney. "I've got it, princess." Her cheeks pink at the nickname, and I find that I enjoy seeing her flushed that way.

Everyone sits down, Kent and Nick taking the seats on either side of the table, leaving the ends for Courtney and myself. With everyone seated, I start serving the spaghetti. Nick passes the plate of toast around, and Kent fills everyone's wine glasses. The three of us work really well together, and within moments, the food and drink are passed out.

"Thank you all for joining me tonight. I'm happy that I get to spend more time with you."

KENT

It's obvious that something happened between Courtney and Colin today. They're acting more comfortable around each other. I breathe a contented sigh. Then Courtney clears her throat. "I guess now is as good a time as any. Colin asked me a question earlier, and I felt like it would be better to explain everything once instead of multiple times."

Colin holds up his hand. "You don't have to talk about it if you don't want to, princess. I was just being nosey."

She shakes her head. "It's okay. You should know, especially with everything that's happened today." Court takes a sip of wine and continues. "Colin asked me why I don't have a pack. I don't like to talk about it, but I almost did have one. I lived in New York for a couple of years, and while I was there, I dated a man named Chad and his pack. He was not a kind alpha, and expected omegas to be subservient. When he realized that wasn't me, he got violent. That's what triggered my anxiety attack earlier. Colin's anger at me being in your home set me off."

"That wasn't—I'm sorry." He looks at her, guilt written all over his face.

"It's okay. I understand that there was more to it than just that. But it took me back to that place, and I didn't deal with it well. Which brings me to the next thing I have to apologize for. In less than ten hours, I've kissed two of you. I don't want to drive a wedge between you. I'd like for us to be friends." She pauses, waiting for someone to be angry with her.

"What if we want more than that?" I can't believe I just said that out loud. But if she kissed me and Colin, then she's obviously interested, right?

"I don't know. I'm not sure I'm ready for that," she admits.

"We're not going to push you, honey," Nick assures her. I hate how timid she's acting right now. How could that asshole have done this to her? I want to find him and destroy him. But I can't do that. She's not mine to defend. No matter how much I want her to be.

"We can take things slow and get to know each other first. Start as friends and see where it goes," Colin adds.

Their soft words seem to relax her. "Do you mean that? What happens if I'm never ready for more?" A tear slides down her cheek and Nick presses his palm to her cheek, wiping it away with his thumb.

"None of us will ever force you into anything, sweetheart. We would love to explore a relationship with you as our omega, but if that's not something you want, then we would never push you or take advantage." I'm compelled to reassure her. I want to pull her into my arms and comfort her, but I think that would scare her away right now.

NICK

"How can you guys promise that?" she asks, her voice trembling.

I take her hand and pull her toward me. She stands and takes two steps toward me. I tug again and she doesn't resist. I scoot my chair back and ease her onto my lap. "We can promise that because we have the ability to control ourselves." I rub my hand along her back.

"I'm scared," she admits. I can tell that Kent and Colin are struggling because they want to comfort her. But this is my turn.

"It's okay to be scared. I get scared too. But you can't let it interfere with going after what you want. Let's do this together. We'll take things as slowly as you want. And if you decide it's not working out, you just have to tell us and we'll go back to just being friends." It's the best compromise I can offer her, and I hope that she'll agree.

"For example, right now, you're sitting on Nick's lap," Kent starts. "If that makes you uncomfortable, you just have to tell him. No one is going to make you do anything that you don't want."

"But that does mean you'll have to use your words, princess. We aren't mind readers." Colin's voice is harsh, but Courtney doesn't flinch at it.

"Are you sure?" she asks, looking at each of us.

I nod and smile. "I am. One hundred percent. Since the moment we met." Kent and Colin agree. I'm surprised at how easily Colin adds his agreement. That must have been one hell of a conversation earlier. Or one hell of a kiss. Either way, things are going exactly the way I'd hoped they would.

I mean, ideally, I would have already gotten to kiss Courtney, but I'm happy to wait until she's ready. I meant it when I told her we won't push. I rub my hand up and down her back, slowly, in comforting circles.

I can see the tension leave her body as she relaxes into me. "So, how would this work?" Ah, good. She's curious. That's a good first step.

"What if we started dating? Easy, no pressure outings that include all of us, or one-on-one, whichever you want. That way we can get to know each other without any pressure. You're in charge of how fast things move." Kent's suggestion comes so easily that I'm sure he's been debating this since we met her.

It's nice to get confirmation that I know my lovers so well. I knew that both he and Colin were attracted to her that first day. I could see her being our omega then, even if they were hesitant. Courtney looks at Colin and he nods. She's worried about him. It's sweet, and I feel myself fall a little more with the gesture.

"Okay. I think maybe a mixture would be good. Some group dates and some individual. Is that okay?" There she goes hesitating again.

Six

Come Work with Us

COLIN

A couple of weeks after we had dinner with Courtney, I finally have a chance to talk to Kent and Nick about my idea. "Hey, you guys got a minute?"

"We have to go meet the realtor in half an hour," Kent says.

"In other words, yes, we have time. What's up?" Nick adds. It's sweet that he knows when I need to be the focus, and lets it happen. Or makes it happen, either way.

"I think we should hire Courtney. She's already studying exactly what we're doing. It would help her with classes and assignments, and it would help us. She knows this town like no one else. And I have it on good authority that she could use the money." There. I said it all and can't take it back now.

"Don't you think that would be a little odd for us to start dating her then offer her a job?" Kent argues. I know he's just trying to make sure that we're not doing anything unethical, but his rejection of my idea stings a little.

"She's qualified and capable. Why does it matter who she's dating?" I will defend this idea.

"What if you offer the job and she says no?" Nick asks. He doesn't sound like he disagrees, though.

"Then we talk her into it. I think we need her for the big project. Everything will go faster with extra hands to code it." I know I'm pushing, but I can't think of another way to help her make enough money to pay her bills. Even if we just pay her to finish her classes and give her a break that way.

"I can see you're set on this. How about a compromise? We can offer her a chance to apply for a job and see what she says. I don't want her to feel like she has to accept a job because she's dating us or that she has to date us to get the job. Do you understand my hesitation?" Kent cups my cheek and presses a gentle kiss to my lips.

"I do. I'm just worried about her," I admit.

"Wow, you went from asshole to best friend in two seconds flat," Nick teases. I hang my head for a minute. I know that I treated her poorly the first couple of times we met, and I regret that.

"Maybe I'm just trying to make up for that. And she told me that missing work the other day because of her thumb really messed with her finances. I really want to help. I didn't like the way that made me feel, thinking that she won't be able to pay her bills."

"What if we write it in the contract that our personal relationship will have no bearing on our business one? Wouldn't that keep things ethical?" Nick is finally on my side. I can see Kent starting to waver.

"We can make an offer. But don't get upset if she refuses."

NICK

The meeting with Sharon, the realtor, goes quickly with no issues. I never doubted that the owners would take our offer, since it was twenty thousand over their asking price. I guess that must be a small-town thing. They don't want to take advantage of anyone, so they price things low. It keeps the cost of living down, but it also undervalues their property.

I was touched when Kent made the offer, especially since the owners are an elderly couple who were selling the property so they could move to Arizona and be closer to family. We helped them reach that goal. Sharon gives us the keys to the building, along with our copy of the contract, and a box of fresh baked cookies. "Ethel baked these for you boys this morning. Her peanut butter cookies are award winning around here. None of you are allergic, are you? I didn't think to ask before."

I shake my head. "No, we don't have any allergies. Thank you. And please let Ethel know how much we appreciate the gesture."

"Well, I won't keep you. I know you boys have a lot of work to do to get the building ready for your business. Maybe Courtney can help with the construction. You know that girl is a whiz with a hammer." I think it's sweet how everyone in this town recommends each other and pushes business to their friends.

"We're planning to ask for her assistance later today. Thank you for the recommendation. I should get going. We do have a lot to do. Thanks again." I walk out the door with the box of cookies and paperwork tucked under my arm, and the keys securely in my pocket.

Kent is filing paperwork that will allow us to make renovations, so I head to the courthouse to pick him up. It was easier to split up and handle different things between the three of us. Colin is discussing our rather large order with Earl at the hardware store. Hopefully he has that handled.

I walk into the office that handles business permits and see Kent. He looks mildly annoyed, so I walk over. "What's up?"

"They don't want to let us make the updates we need to. The building is historical and has to stay the same structurally. I don't know if we can make it work without the changes we had planned."

I think for a second before responding. "We should talk to Courtney and see what she thinks. There may be some cosmetic changes that could take the place of the structural ones. Would they let us do those instead?"

Kent kisses me hard, then turns back to the lady that's approaching us. "You're brilliant," he whispers over his shoulder. I can't help but smile at that.

"I'm sorry, Mr. Olsen. There's nothing we can do. The structure of the building has to stay the same."

"What if we bring in Harris Contracting to make sure the structure remains intact?" he asks her.

She nods. "I think that could work."

COURTNEY

My phone rings, and I pull it out of my pocket without looking at who's calling. "Court here. What can I help with?"

"Can you meet us at the property on main street? We need to talk to you about a job," Kent insists.

"I can be there in fifteen minutes. Is everything okay?" I'll have to finish up with Mrs. Henderson's bathroom sink, but that shouldn't take much longer.

"Not really. They won't let us make any structural changes to the building, but it won't work the way it is right now. We need your help." I can hear the panic in his voice. And I'm sure that Martha made it sound like there was nothing they could do.

"I'll be there in fifteen. It's gonna be okay. We'll figure out a way to make it work. Okay?" I wait for his confirmation to hang up. Then I refocus on the two pipes I'm fitting together. With that complete, I let Mrs. H know that I'll check back tomorrow to be sure the seal is holding. Then I hurried to meet the guys.

This town is so uptight about historical buildings that it isn't funny. There's a list of rules for renovations that's a mile long at least. And he's not wrong that we won't be able to make structural changes. That doesn't mean we can't find a compromise. I know these people like the back of my hand. I can find a way to make things work for them.

I park the truck, grabbing a tape measure, a pencil, and a notepad. I tuck the pencil into my ponytail, the notebook in my back pocket, and clip the tape to my waistband. I stop outside the building and try to imagine what the guys want it to look like.

My ability to see the finished product helps me with things like this. I can see the best option for updates, while keeping the building's structure intact. I pull out the notepad and pencil and jot down some notes before tucking them away again and walking up to the door. Nick meets me with a huge grin and a big hug.

"Hey there, stranger," he says with a laugh. I just saw them this morning when everyone was leaving for the day.

"Long time no see," I retort. He laughs at my joke. "He's freaking out, huh?"

Nick nods. "Yeah, worse than usual. Please help."

"I've got this. Show me the changes you want to make, and we'll see what we can do to work them around the building's structure. I'm sure there's a way to make it work."

Kent walks over with blueprints and spreads them over a folding table. He explains everything and I jot down a few more notes. Then I take them around the entire building, discussing alternatives to what they'd planned, and pointing out places where their plans could stand as they are.

"You're a lifesaver. I thought they weren't going to let us do anything to it. But this is way more than I expected," Kent sighed in relief.

"Yeah, it's not as bad as I thought either. The only thing you can't do is remove that wall. But there are things we can do to open up that space if you need it." I've been measuring, taking notes, and explaining things about the historical building re-strictions for an hour now.

"So, you'll take the job? We'll help with it all, but we don't know enough about the town's code to do this ourselves." Nick is bouncing around the whole time, and I didn't think he was paying any attention.

I'm not sure if I should be working for the guys I'm dating, but I don't know how they'll get this accomplished without me. "If we have a very specific contract with wording that protects both parties, yes." I don't want to offend them, but I also don't want them to think that I'm taking advantage of them, either.

"Great! I'll get that drawn up." Nick bounces away again, pulling out a laptop and ducking into another room.

"He's so full of energy," I chuckle.

"If only you knew," Kent laughs. I like how well we're all getting along right now, but I worry that mixing business with pleasure will screw it all up.

"Actually, there was something else we wanted to talk to you about if you have another moment," he says, drawing my attention back to him.

"I'm done for the day, so I have time. What can I help with?" I sense that he's hesitating, but I have no idea why. My heart starts to race and I have to take a deep breath to calm myself.

Kent must notice that I'm nervous. He takes my hand and walks me over to a couple of folding chairs next to the table with the blueprints. "It's nothing bad. Please don't freak out. We've been talking."

Shit. Here it comes. We like you, but we've decided we don't really want to be with you. I should be relieved, because it means we'll be able to work together without any chance of things getting messy. But I can't stop my disappointment from showing.

"And we'd like to give you the chance to apply for a job with us. If you're interested. No pressure. But what we do is directly lined up with your classes, and we thought that one could help the other. You'd get practical experience while you finish the classes, and you'd get a decent paycheck at the same time. Again, no pressure, it's just a thought," he explains.

"Wow, that is not what I expected you to say," I admit.

"What did you think I was going to say?" he asks. I feel my cheeks turn crimson and duck my head.

"That you guys talked and decided you don't want to date me after all."

KENT

Courtney's whispered words floor me. "How could you think that's what I was going to say? Did we do something to make you think we don't want to be with you?"

She shakes her head. "No, you didn't. I've just learned to expect the worst, you know?"

I pull her into my lap. "There is nothing you could do to make us not want to be with you. The only way we'll stop pursuing a relationship is if you tell us that you don't want it. And even then, we'd still want you. But we would respect your feelings and back off. Is that what you want?"

She shakes her head again. "Not at all. I just thought maybe you guys were already tired of moving so slow." We've been on a handful of dates over the past couple of weeks, and I've enjoyed every moment.

"Well, that's a relief," I say, pulling her closer and pressing my lips to hers. I'm not pushing for anything, just reassuring, so it's a quick kiss. "I'd hate to think you were that easy to scare away."

"If anything was going to do that, it would be the fact that Nick hasn't kissed me yet," she teases. I knew he was holding out as long as possible, but I would have expected him to give in already.

"Really? That's not like him. Do you want me to talk to him?" I offer, even though I'm convinced that she won't.

"No. He's being really sweet. He says he wants to get to know me first. It's frustrating, but I'm sure there are things I do that frustrate you all as well. I'm sure it'll be worth the wait. And it's not like I know when it'll happen, so that makes things even more interesting." I'm glad that she's not disappointed, and that everyone is being respectful of boundaries.

This relationship has already lasted longer than the one with Terri, so I'm fairly confident that even Colin has relaxed. Courtney stands up and walks the few steps to the table. "You didn't answer me, you know." I don't want to push, but I want to know if she's at least interested in joining the company. If things work out the way we want, she'll be part owner soon enough.

Not that she'd let us take care of her. She's too independent for that. But it's one of the things I love about her. I watch her as she contemplates the offer while staring at the blueprints.

"Are you sure about this? You guys really want me around you that much? I don't want you to get sick of me," she counters.

"We're sure. And we can work it out so we're not all on top of each other all the time, if that makes you more comfortable. We'll require you to complete your classes while working, so you'll basically be paid to learn."

"That's a very generous offer. Can I think it over?"

Seven

Small Town Gossip

NICK

I'm not sure what happened while I was drawing up the contract for Court to help us with the renovations, but both she and Kent are acting weird when I come back. "Okay, here's the contract. Take a look at it and if everything is right, we can set up a time to get it all notarized."

I hand her the papers I've just printed. "Thanks. I should go so I can read over this. I'll let you know what I decide."

Something is definitely wrong here. I give Kent a look, but he just nods at her. What the fuck? I follow her out the door.

"Court, wait," I call to get her attention.

She stops just outside the door, but doesn't say anything. "Are you okay? Did Kent do something to upset you?"

"It's fine, Nick. I just need some time to process everything." Her response does little to calm my nerves.

"Did I do something wrong?" Now I'm worried that she's changing her mind about us, and I don't want that.

"No. The job offers are just a lot to take in with everything else going on." She doesn't look at me when she answers.

"Job offers, like plural? He wasn't supposed to spring that on you yet. But if you mean with us dating? I promise the contracts will be completely on the level. Everyone's interests will be protected. Please don't give up on us because we know that you're the best person for the job." I take a step closer and reach for her hand.

"It's not that. I just don't want it to look like I'm only dating you for a job. Or that you only hired me because we're dating. You guys don't really know how small towns work. People will talk." She looks down at our joined hands as if to make her point.

I step forward and pull her into my arms. "Then let them talk." I'd been waiting for the perfect moment for our first kiss. This isn't it, but I'm feeling a little bit desperate to get my message across. She needs to know that we don't care who knows we're dating.

I tease my lips against hers for a moment, testing to see her reaction. She moans and I take advantage, slipping my tongue in and stroking it along hers. I wrap my arms around her tighter as she deepens the kiss.

I lose myself in the sensation of her pressed against me. I kiss her as if my life depends on that contact. Maybe it does.

When she finally pulls away, we're both breathless and flushed. There's nothing like standing in front of your new business location and making out with your girl. I notice people across the street whispering, but I don't care.

Courtney's cheeks turn red and she dashes toward her truck. Did I just fuck this up? I turn around and head back inside.

"What happened with Court after I left?" I ask Kent casually, as if I haven't already figured it out.

COURTNEY

Everything today is just too much. Kent's job offers; Nick's admission that they don't care who knows that we're dating. My desire to give in and take the job with them just to make things easier on myself isn't helping. I know that they respect me and value my abilities, but I can't help thinking that this offer is just because we've started dating.

And what if things don't work out? Then will I be out a job? I'm not sure I can risk that, no matter how badly I want the job. It doesn't help that Mary and Susie saw Nick kiss me. That'll be all over town within the hour. I can't go home, because I'll have to face the guys. I can't go to the diner, because everyone will be talking about that kiss.

My only other option is to drive out to the lake and hide while I think things through. I don't want to hide. I don't want to be embarrassed that a sexy man kissed me in public. But we've just started dating and I have no idea where this is going. I know exactly where I want it to go, though. So, I drive out to the lake and back the truck in.

I lay in the bed of the truck, where I can stare at the water and try to figure my life out. It's strange that I feel like I'm spiraling, when there are three amazing men who are interested in me, who just happen to own the company that contains my dream job. Why is this such a big deal to me?

Would it really hurt to take the job? So what if people talk? I hate the idea of people thinking I've used my body to get work. That's why I can't do it. I can't let my integrity be compromised that way. I need to keep things professional in my professional life. But what good does that do when I can't pay the bills?

I need to figure this out. I can't keep doing what I'm doing now. I can't raise my prices, because people wouldn't be able to afford it if I did. But I can't live on what they're paying. Fuck. I don't really know what to do here. My phone rings, pulling me from my thoughts. I look at it, prepared to ignore the call. But I can't, because it's Mama.

"Hi," I answer.

"Kiddo, what in the world is going on? I heard that a handsome fella kissed you today and you ran away. Are you okay?" Of course, someone called her and told her about it.

"Yes, I'm fine. I mean, I'm not okay at all, but it doesn't have as much to do with that fella as you'd think. At least, not the kiss. That was great. Sorry, I'm rambling," I say, giving her a chance to talk.

"Baby girl. You sound stressed. So, the fella didn't force himself on you? If he's not the problem, why don't you tell me what is? Take a deep breath and get your thoughts together so I can follow." Mama always did know how to get me talking.

I take a deep breath, as instructed, and start at the beginning. "Well, as you already know from the gossip queens, I'm dating someone. Three someones, actually. They're great guys, and they just moved into the Johnson house next door."

"Oh, those boys! Yes, they are nice boys. Good choice."

"Well, in addition to that, they own OBP Tech. And they've asked me to come work for them." I wait for her reaction.

"I don't see the problem, Court. Unless they only offered the job because you're sleeping with them. Then that's a problem," Mama insists.

"I'm not sleeping with them. At least not yet. We're taking things slow because of Chad. And they've had some issues as well. But won't the entire town think that they only hired me because of our relationship?" My heart starts to race again and my stomach flips.

"My sweet girl. You can't live your life worrying about what other people think. Will there be some gossips around town that talk? Yes. Does that matter? No. Honey, you have to do what you feel is right. If this job is what you want to do, you should take it. And if you care about these boys, you should try to make it work. There are risks in any relationship, business or personal. Only you can decide if these opportunities are worth it or not." When Mama is finished, I have tears streaming down my face. She's right, as usual.

"Thank you. I needed someone to give it to me straight. I just hope I haven't messed up too much for them to forgive me. I really like them, Mama. And I'm sure you would too."

I can hear the sweet smile in her voice. "I'm sure I will, when I finally get to meet them. Your dad and I will come visit during the summer when it's warm. I'll let you go, since you have some things to consider. I love you, kiddo."

"I love you, too, Mama. We'll talk soon." I disconnect the call and lay my phone on my stomach. She's right about everything. I have a lot of thinking to do. I need to figure out how this could possibly work. Because I really want it to.

When my phone rings again, I glance at it, but don't answer. I just can't talk to Nick right now. I know that I hurt his feelings by running away. I'll have to figure out how to make it up to him. But I can't think about that right now. I need to get my anxiety under control so I can accept the job offer and fight through the fear that's threatening to weigh me down.

KENT

I'm shocked when Courtney runs away from the job offer. I hope that after she takes some time to think about it, she'll accept. We could really use her help. But we promised her that we won't push her into anything she doesn't want. And that includes job offers.

Nick storms back into the office after he chases after her. "What happened with Court after I left?" he asks. I drop my head and stare at the floor.

"I fucked up. I made the other job offer without thinking that it may be too much for her all at once. I can fix it; she just needs some time to process." I raise my head to meet his gaze.

"She's pretty upset. And now the gossip queens are talking, because for some reason, I thought it would be a good idea to kiss her on the street in front of them. So, you're not the only one who fucked up," he replies.

I walk over and pull him into my arms. "It's okay. We'll fix it. What can we do to fix it?" I press a kiss to the top of his head.

"Shakes from the diner? That might help. Unless she's really pissed at us. Then it's gonna take more than ice cream to make this better. I thought that I'd pushed her away, and that kissing her would help her understand how I feel. Now I feel like an ass."

We stand there, just holding each other for a while. "Well, we can't just stand here and dwell on our mistakes. We need to get moving before this gets worse. Ice cream?" I ask.

"Ice cream," Nick responds.

We lock up and head to the diner for shakes. Ms. Gertrude is at the counter when we walk in, and I notice that it gets strangely quiet when we approach her. "What can I get for you boys?" she asks. For some reason, she doesn't seem as friendly as the last time we were here.

"We'd like to get four shakes, please." Nick turns to me. "What flavor does she like?"

Ms. Gertrude eyes us suspiciously. "If you're talking about Courtney, she likes the chocolate peanut butter cup shake. You boys have been spending a lot of time with her lately, haven't you?"

Ah, here's the gossip mill at work now. "Yes, ma'am, we have. As a matter of fact, our pack is courting her. But we're taking things slow because we want to get to know each other. Do you have a problem with that?" I look around at the people who were whispering when we walked in. From their embarrassed expressions, I know they were talking about us.

"We're also trying to get her to come work for us at our company. She's smart and capable, but perhaps a little too concerned with your opinion of her choices." I shouldn't have said it, but now that it's out, I won't apologize.

Every one of them looks ashamed, as they should.

COLIN

Nick and Kent get home and I can tell something is wrong. "Court won't answer my calls," Nick says. They hand me a milkshake and put one in the fridge. Since they each have one, I'm guessing that one is for our missing girl.

"Did you piss her off?" I ask, teasing him. Then I see the tears starting to fill his eyes, and I feel bad. I drag him against me and kiss him deeply. "It's okay, love. Tell me what happened and we'll fix it."

After Nick and Kent explain what happened with Court and at the diner, I start to worry. She's a grown woman, yes, but it sounds like she was pretty upset. Then I think of something she told me the other day. "I think I know where she is. Come on."

I load them into the car and take off for the lake that my princess told me about. I remember the directions clearly, and within a few minutes, I'm parking the car next to her truck. It's a beautiful place to hide. And it's obvious that's what she's doing. "Wait here, please," I order before getting out.

I walk to the back of her truck and our eyes meet. "May I join you?" I ask, waiting until she nods to climb in the truck bed with her. "You wanna talk about it?"

"I did. With my mom. I just needed a little while to process everything. I hurt Nick's feelings and I have to make it up to him," she explains as a tear falls down her cheek. I scoot over next to her and wrap my arms around her.

"Princess, it's okay. There will be hurt feelings sometimes, and misunderstandings. It's perfectly acceptable to feel whatever you feel. But you can't just disappear, especially after telling us what little you did about Chad. We were worried. Because we care about you." I rub my hand down her back as I speak, letting her cry into my chest.

"I know. I'm sorry. It was all just too much, and I needed to breathe. Then I talked to Mama, and I felt even worse because I screwed up. I was worried that you guys wouldn't want me anymore."

How could she ever think we wouldn't want her because of a simple misunderstanding? "Oh, princess. I'm sorry you felt that way. I hope you know now that it would take more than this to make us not want to be with you. Can the guys join us? I think snuggles are in order." She nods at my request and I throw a hand up to motion for them to come over.

Kent climbs up first, helping Nick into the truck bed. I pull Court over to the middle so Nick can sit next to her. Kent settles beside me. "I'm sorry. I reacted poorly to everything."

She grabs Nick and kisses him while I'm still holding her. Then she turns and kisses Kent, and finally me.

Eight

A Date to Remember

COURTNEY

AFTER OUR ALMOST BREAK up, the guys insist on taking me out for Valentine's Day. I didn't realize it was this week, so I'm feeling completely unprepared. They promise to take it easy on me. I know that they're used to eating at fancy restaurants and going out in LA. That's a little different from what we have to offer here in Indiana.

All I know is that we're going to dinner and I need to wear something comfortable but nice. I decide on some sexy black lingerie under my slinky maroon dress. It's not the most comfortable thing I own, but it'll definitely get their attention. I'm ready early, and I know that I should wait for the guys to pick me up, but I can't handle the anticipation.

I slip out of my heels and cross the yard. I'll put them back on when we're ready to go. I knock, and smirk when Nick opens the door. His eyes go wide, and his jaw drops. I don't wear dresses often, but this seems like the right choice. I step forward, closing his mouth by lifting his chin, before pressing my lips to his.

"You look amazing," he stammers, stepping back so I can come inside. "Kent and Colin are just about ready. We were going to pick you up."

"I know. I got bored waiting." I smirk at him again.

"Sure you did." He laughs. "You just wanted to see my reaction to that dress." He's not wrong.

"You clean up nice too," I tease him, running my hand along his tie, then using it to pull him to me for another kiss. "Can we just stay home instead?"

"I'm all for that, but no. You agreed to dinner. Kent made reservations, and Colin is actually pretty excited about this. Don't ruin it." Being admonished by my usually happy alpha doesn't make me happy.

"Sorry. I had to try. I'm not used to going out to fancy dinners," I admit. I can't tell them that I'm feeling nervous that I'll embarrass them at the restaurant. As many times as Chad made me feel like a worthless hick, I hate admitting that to anyone.

Nick wraps his arms around me. "I promise this isn't a really fancy place. Dinner will be a few courses, but it's not anything uppity." His words and closeness soothe me. His sweet chocolate scent relaxes me and makes it easier to breathe.

A flash of desire courses through me. None of us has pushed the issue, but I hope we're getting closer to finally having sex. All three guys have been more than patient with me about my past trauma. I want to move things forward, but I don't want to freak out the first time one of them really touches me.

I guess there's no way to know what will happen until we get there. And if the way Nick looks at me is any indication, that will be very soon.

NICK

Courtney's dress is perfection. I'm so used to seeing her in jeans and t-shirts that I almost don't recognize her. It's all I can do to keep from making a move on her. I hold myself back, because Kent went to a lot of trouble to get these reservations, and she promised us a real date. It's Valentine's Day, after all. That's it! I'll distract her with the cheesy gift I got her.

"Wait right here," I request, then race up the stairs to my room to grab the cute little plush kitten. I hope she likes it. I run down the stairs and barely stop myself from falling into her when I stop. "This is for you. Close your eyes and hold out your hands."

She does as I ask, and I put the plush in her hands. Her eyes open and I can see the excitement in them. "It's so cute and soft. Thank you!" Then her face falls and I see a hint of sadness. "I didn't get you guys anything."

"That's okay. You didn't have to."

"But I feel bad now," she pouts.

I take her hand and pull her close to me. "I can think of something you can give me that I would happily count as my gift." As soon as I say it, I know that there are two ways she can take that. Hopefully she doesn't think I'm talking about sex. I'd love that, but I'm not going to use that tactic to get there.

She looks at me skeptically. "What's that?"

"A kiss."

"You'd be happy with a kiss as a gift? Why do I feel like that's not what you meant?" She leans forward anyway and presses her lips to mine. I want to deepen the kiss and take things as far as she's comfortable with, but a promise is a promise. I will not push her for anything more than she's ready for.

When she breaks contact, I glare at her. "You don't believe me because you're a dirty pervert." I can't keep a straight face and we both laugh at the same time.

We stand there for a while, with my arms barely around her, my fingers tracing her waist and back. "I really like this dress," I tell her.

"Thanks. It's new." Her statement makes me think that she bought it just for tonight. Part of me hopes that she did.

Before I can respond, Kent comes down the stairs. "Oh, sweetheart, you look absolutely delicious." He walks over and presses a kiss to her cheek.

"Don't you look handsome?" she responds. I relinquish my hold on her and let him pull her into his arms. I hear Colin's footsteps and turn toward the stairs, giving them a moment of privacy.

"Did I hear Court? I thought we were picking her up." Colin comes down the stairs, stopping as soon as he sees her. "Wow."

I glance at her and smile at the blush that covers her cheeks.

KENT

All three of my loves look gorgeous tonight. I almost don't want to go to the restaurant, but it took forever to find the right one. So, I load everyone up into the car and we're on our way. It's a short drive to the next town over. Within a little while, we're seated and have ordered.

I catch movement over Courtney's shoulder, and do a double take. It's not possible. I want to get Nick's attention and have him look, but I can't do that without Colin and Court seeing too. And if this is who I think, neither of them needs to deal with it tonight. Just as I convince myself that I'm wrong, the waitress comes back with our drink orders. I've opted to be the driver tonight, so I'm just having soda while the others have a glass of wine.

The first course of our dinner is fondue with toast squares. The gooey, melty cheese tastes as good as my dates look. I can't help looking again for the woman I saw. I would almost swear it was her. But there's no way. It can't be. Can it?

"Kent? Are you okay? You seem distracted," Courtney says, waving her hand in front of my face to get my attention. Fuck.

"Yeah, I'm fine. Sorry." I know it's a flimsy apology, but I try my best to refocus and pay attention to the conversation.

The next course comes out, and the salad is delicious. It has an Italian dressing and is loaded with veggies. Colin makes a face, but at least picks at it. I catch myself staring at the woman across the restaurant and I swear that it's her. I don't want to alert the others, so I know I have to stop staring at her. Besides, Courtney is so much better to look at.

Fear grips my heart. If it is her, we could be in danger. I'll never forgive myself if something were to happen to any of my dates because I couldn't protect them from this monster. I pull my eyes back to our table. I have to stop staring. But I can feel her eyes on me, and I'm sure now that it's her. I have to find a way to call for help without alerting her.

She can't get arrested again if she flees the scene. I can't believe I thought we'd managed to escape her when she was locked up and we moved across the country. Of course, she somehow followed us and found out where we are.

Court reaches across the table and rubs my hand. "Are you okay? You seem upset now. Is everything okay with dinner?"

I want to tell her, but I can't force the words out. She deserves to know what has me on edge, as do Colin and Nick. But I can't make myself say it. I don't want to believe it. What do I do?

COURTNEY

Kent is acting really strange. He keeps staring past me, as if he's seen a ghost. At first, I think something is wrong with our dinner. Then I realize that he sees someone he recognizes here and it terrifies him. My experience with Chad pushes to the front of my memories, and I'm sure I had that look on my face a few times after I left him. Terri is here. I don't know much about her, except that she tried to kill them when they turned her down as a packmate. I thought she was still in jail.

"I need to use the ladies' room. I'll be right back," I excuse myself from the table. I glance over my shoulder as soon as I'm behind Kent. Sure enough, there's a woman staring at our table. That has to be her. What the fuck am I going to do about it?

I refuse to let her ruin what we're building here. I glare at her on my way back from the restroom. Then I make it a point to kiss Colin, Kent, and Nick before I sit back down. To top it off, I smirk at her after I do it. That should get her moving. I won't attack someone in a crowded restaurant, but I will fight back if she comes at us.

"What was that for?" Kent asks as I slide back into my chair.

I put my hand over his on the table. "I know. Don't worry, I've got this."

It takes a moment, but realization washes over him, and the other two look at us funny. "What are you two talking about?"

Before I can answer, my head is jerked back and I'm whipped around to face the short, chubby woman who must be the menace my guys told me about. I hear their gasps, but I have complete control of this situation. I knock her hand from my hair.

"Get your hands off me and take a step back. If I'm not mistaken, there's a restraining order against you. I'd appreciate it if you'd remove yourself from the area before I have to take matters into my own hands." My voice is cold and harsh. I can feel the tension hanging in the air. But one deep breath and I'm completely calm. It's as if Kent's caramel scent wraps around me, mixing with Nick's chocolate, and Colin's cherries. Just for me.

"You bitch. These are my men. They're my pack. You can take your slut ass out the door. I'm not leaving." She's making a scene even before she raises the steak knife at me. What is it with crazy bitches and steak knives?

I don't give her the chance to stab me or one of my guys. My fists shoots out and slams into her nose, knocking her head back. She drops the knife and covers her face as blood pours from it.

COLIN

My jaw drops at seeing Terri again. I watch her try to fight with Courtney. I don't know what I'll do if Terri hurts her. My heart races and my hands are like ice. Then Courtney breaks Terri's nose, and I see Kent calling the police. I start to laugh because I don't know what else to do. It's not funny at all, and I'm terrified that somehow Terri will attack Court and we'll lose her.

I'm frozen in place as I watch our omega take out her wanna-be competition. At this moment, I have no idea what I ever saw in Terri. She's an ugly person who only ever wanted to control us. She hated the fact that I had relationships with Kent and Nick. She wanted everyone focused on her. But Court is the opposite of that. She seems to enjoy our easy affection.

I watch as Terri drops her hands from her face, deciding to attack, since there was nothing that she could do about her nose. I stand up, but Court shakes her head. "I've got this. It's fine."

Terri punches her in the eye, but Court doesn't react. Instead, she throws a left-right combo and Terri hits the ground.

I'm shocked. I had no idea that Courtney knew how to fight. Relief washes over me when a large man walks over and drags Terri up from the floor. He secures her hands with zip ties and escorts her away to wait for the police.

"Well, that was fun." Court brushes her hands off and turns to the restaurant manager, who came to see what was going on. Kent explains the situation to him, and he apologizes profusely for the interruption of our dinner. I'm pretty sure none of us will be eating anymore tonight. We apologize to the other diners, but everyone saw what happened. Every table applauds Courtney and tells us that she did a great job. It's ridiculous, but I love it. She deserves the recognition.

When everyone leaves us alone again, I reach for her. She seems to understand that I need comfort and lets me pull her onto my lap. "Thank you for that, princess. I'm sorry I froze up when I saw she was here."

Court grabs my face and kisses me again. "Colin, I understand. You guys were traumatized by that crazy bitch. I don't mind taking care of you."

"I didn't believe it was her at first," Kent says quietly. "If I had said something, we could have been more prepared."

"Don't blame yourself, either. I took care of it. I hope that doesn't offend you guys. I just wanted to protect you," she sounds ashamed now. Because she feels like she overstepped. Fuck.

"Princess, you have nothing to apologize for. You did what we couldn't. There's no way we could have punched her or physically attacked her at all."

Nick takes her hand. "That was awesome. You're so fucking hot when you beat up crazy women."

Nine

An Unexpected Heat

KENT

I'M STILL BEATING MYSELF up for not saying something about Terri being here. Because I second-guessed myself, none of us feel like finishing dinner. "I'm sorry the night was ruined. We don't have to stay," I offer. It would be bad enough if it were just me, Nick, and Colin, but for it to impact our first big date with Courtney upsets me to no end.

"We can go home and watch a movie or something. Order pizza if we get hungry later," Nick suggests. Court and Colin nod. So much for our fancy date. But at least she's not running away from us. I would hate for Terri to have chased her off.

We load up into the car and head home. "Is it hot in here?" Courtney asks when we get about halfway home. I turn the heat down, but glance at Nick.

He shakes his head and looks at Colin, who also shakes his head. The middle of February in Indiana is anything but warm. Colin leans forward and touches Court's forehead. "She's burning up."

"Are you feeling okay, honey?" Nick asks her with wide eyes.

"Not really. It's so hot in here, and my stomach is cramping." She pauses, then looks out the window. When she faces me again, there are tears streaking her cheeks. "I think I'm going into heat."

The quiet admission is enough to make me drive faster. We have to get her home and take care of her. We pull up to her house and manage to get her inside. "Do you want us to stay with you?" I can't assume that she wants our help with her heat, since we haven't fully discussed this yet.

"Please don't leave me. My nest is upstairs." Her request is a relief. I'd been a little worried that she'd change her mind about us after Terri's interruption tonight.

"I'll get snacks and water," Colin says, heading to the kitchen. I scoop Courtney up into my arms and carry her up the stairs, following her directions to her room, where her nest is.

"Um, before I let you guys in here, I need to tell you something," she insists as I open the door and walk inside. I don't wait for her to say what she's leading up to, heading straight into the small room that holds her nest.

It's strange, but the room smells like us already. How is that possible? "Did you steal our clothes?" I can't help but ask, and I know she's going to get upset.

Nick breaks in before Courtney can respond. "I got them for her. She needed us to be close by, and I understand that." Court's cheeks are bright red, and I'm sure it's not from being warm.

"Okay. We can talk about that later. Let's focus on what Courtney needs right now," I offer. I don't know if I'm flattered or offended that Nick helped her take some of our clothes.

NICK

With the awkward nest situation handled, Kent and I help Court get comfortable. Her nest is filled with fluffy pillows and soft blankets. I know things are moving way too fast, but she's overheating and in pain. I can't handle that, but consent is important. "Honey, I can help ease the pain, but I need to undress you first. Is that okay?"

She whimpers, but I can't take that as a yes. "Sweetheart, we need you to tell us that this is what you want. We don't want to do anything you don't want." Kent's quiet words push her to speak.

"Please take care of me. You have my permission to do whatever needs to be done. Just make the pain stop," she begs. I don't need more than that, so I start to strip off her dress. The sight of her in sexy, strappy black lingerie underneath the dress is almost more than I can take.

I hum my approval as Kent helps me fight with the straps to get her naked. As soon as we get her completely undressed, a shiver washes over her body and goosebumps pepper her skin. I know it's a good start, but she needs more than that to feel better. I drop to my knees in front of her and take her in with my eyes. Her body is stunning. I rest my hands on her knees, then slide them up her thighs as I settle in on my target.

The closer I get to her core, the more she squirms. I look at Kent and nod for him to distract her while I get started. He tilts her face toward him and kisses her gently. At the same time, I slide my tongue along her folds, making her moan into his mouth. I sense Colin as he enters the room, but I don't see him. I lick along her slit again, then suck her clit into my mouth. Her moans get louder as she adjusts to the sensations. I glance up to see Kent and Colin taking turns kissing her while they play with her pebbled nipples.

I know that the only thing that will completely make the pain recede is a knot, but I want to give her some pleasure before we get to that point. I continue to lick and suck at her sweet pussy, then slide a finger inside her. She arches her back and groans. I slip another finger inside and curl them to stroke her g-spot. As I'm working her pussy, Kent and Colin start sucking on her nipples. I flick her clit with my tongue, picking up speed with my fingers, then adding a third.

She stretches easily, her slick lubricating everything. I feel her contract around my fingers as her first orgasm hits. I keep pushing her, drawing a second climax from her before she relaxes enough to tell us what she wants. "That feels so good," she pants. I hum against her mound.

COURTNEY

I don't know what I expected from my first heat, but it definitely wasn't this mind-searing pain. Nick's mouth and fingers help, but not enough. I love the feeling of Kent and Colin sucking and touching me, but it's not enough. I'm so empty, and I'm dying to be full. "I need more," I beg as they continue their assault. I wish we'd had more time to talk about what each of us expect from this. I know the three of them are together, and adding me to that changes things a little.

"Tell us what you need, princess," Colin says in my ear, his breath warm against my skin. In this moment, I believe they would do anything to take care of me. I want them to possess me, to make me theirs. But we didn't really talk about claiming or bonding either.

"I need to be full. I'm so empty. Please," I know I'm begging, but I can't stop myself. I need more than they're giving me, and they won't know unless I tell them.

The three of them exchange a look that tells me that they have discussed this, because in just a moment, Kent and Nick trade places and they all strip down. One of them makes sure to keep touching me as they remove their clothes. I stare at each of them, drinking in their naked bodies. I find myself purring, and it surprises me. It's not a noise I've ever made before.

"Are you sure you're ready?" Kent asks, rubbing his cock at my entrance. I know I'm soaked with slick, and the emptiness hurts so bad.

"Yes, please, alpha. I need your knot." I'm panting with desire, desperate for him to fuck me hard. I know there are so many things we should have talked about, but I thought I had more time. With my quiet admission, he slides into me. Kent's movements are slow at first making me squirm, trying to get him in deeper.

"Take it easy, sweetheart. I don't want to hurt you," he protests. He doesn't understand this pain I'm feeling or how badly I need him to be completely inside me.

"You're not going to. Please. I'm made for this." My voice is rough, but he takes me at my word, sheathing himself inside of me. I call out in surprise. I thought I got a good look at each of them, but I didn't realize how big he is.

Now that Kent is deep inside of me, I start to squirm again. I need him to move. I need the friction to push me over the edge. "More." That one word has Colin moving to help Kent roll onto his back with me on top of him. Then Colin slides two fingers inside of me alongside of Kent's dick. He rubs my slick around my rosebud before dipping a finger inside, then two. He gently stretches me, making sure I'm ready for him. "Yes," I cry out at the sensations. I reach for Nick, guiding his cock into my mouth as Colin slides into my ass.

This is so much better. I finally feel full. The pain in my abdomen eases as they work together, alternating thrusts over and over and leading me to my next orgasm. It doesn't take much encouragement to get Nick to fuck my mouth. I want them to use me for their pleasure, too. This isn't just about me.

I moan around Nick as Kent and Colin push me closer to the edge. The vibration makes Nick move faster, thrusting into my throat hard. I love these sensations so much. I come hard, clamping down on them both as Nick comes down my throat. I swallow over and over, milking him until he starts to soften. I let him pull out of my mouth and he leans down to capture my lips with his, kissing me deep and hard. I pull him close and bite his shoulder, right over his scent gland. Then I turn so I can kiss Colin before I claim him with a bite as well.

I feel Kent's knot swell up with his release, locking us in place. His knot triggers Colin's release, and my own. I don't even know how many times I've come, but the pain is gone for now. Kent rocks his hips, his cock stroking against my g-spot, and I come again, biting Kent to claim him as well. I hadn't planned to claim any of them yet, but I couldn't resist in the moment.

Colin slips out of me as Kent's knot starts to go down. Suddenly, Nick is wiping me down with a warm rag. Colin holds a bottle of water to my lips and I drink deeply.

I feel sated and tired, but Kent insists that I eat something before I sleep. He hand feeds me fruit and cheese until I can't eat anymore. "Thank you." The words seem awkward, but I want them to know that I appreciate them.

"I know there's a lot we haven't talked about, but we're here for you. Whatever you need." I'm not sure which of them says the words, but the three of them look at me so intently. I worry that I shouldn't have bitten them, but they don't look upset.

"I want you to claim me as well," I say breathlessly. "But only if you want. I'm sorry, I should have asked first." I drop my head, staring at the floor. They've been so sweet to me, and I acted rashly. I mentally kick myself for not thinking, even though I acted on instinct. I couldn't think straight at that moment if I had tried.

Instead of responding, Kent licks my neck before sinking his teeth into the skin over my scent gland. I moan at the contact. A moment later, he backs off and Nick claims me with his bite in almost the same spot. Then Colin bites me, since I bit him.

COLIN

I know that my bite does nothing to seal a bond, but since Courtney bit me to claim me, it only seems fair. She moans her approval. I glance at Nick and Kent, but they look pleased, not upset. We hadn't discussed claiming or bonding during Courtney's heat, but I'm glad she forced the issue.

"If you think for a second that we don't want you, then you weren't paying attention," I tell her quietly. She kisses each of us gently, then is asleep within a minute. We snuggle up with her and sleep while we can. When she wakes up, she's going to need us again.

Two full days later, her heat finally subsides. I don't know how many different positions and combinations we went through while taking care of our omega. All I know is that I want more than anything to stay here forever. Everything feels too good to be true, and I worry that I'll screw it up somehow.

Kent, Nick, and I make breakfast for Courtney while she sleeps. We're not great in the kitchen, but together we manage. "I think we need to make things official. Which means we need to get a ring," Nick insists as he stirs the gravy that will go with the biscuits.

"I agree, but how will we manage that without telling her? And what if she says no?" I can't help but feel like it's too much too soon. I prepare myself for rejection so that it doesn't hurt as much.

"I can take care of the ring after breakfast. And if she says no, then we'll deal with that. I don't think she will, since she was the one to initiate the claiming," Kent chimes in. I trust him to select the perfect ring for our omega.

He wraps his arms around me and kisses me lightly. "Don't worry, love. Everything is going to work out this time. She's not like Terri."

I relax against him, letting his words sink in. Courtney walks into the kitchen, smiling from ear to ear. "I was worried that you guys left. But you made breakfast? I didn't think you knew how to cook."

The three of us surround her in a group embrace. "We would never just leave without kissing you goodbye," Nick tells her before pressing his lips to hers. She giggles against his mouth before returning his kiss.

"That's good, because I'd hate to have to kick your asses too," she jokes, clearly referencing her fight with Terri. We groan. "What? Too soon?" she laughs.

I pull her into my arms and kiss her deeply, holding on tightly to this miracle that we've found. When I break the kiss, she puts her hands on my cheeks. "Are you okay? I know that situation was difficult for you, and then my heat. We didn't get to talk about it."

Her concern touches me in a way I haven't felt in a while. "I'm good."

Ten

Epilogue

COURTNEY

I'M NOT SURE THAT I believe Colin when he says that he's good, but I don't push. We've been through a lot in the past few days. At some point, we'll have to talk about the fact that I basically forced them into claiming me while I was in heat. That conversation scares me. What if they didn't want to bond with me in the first place?

I don't voice my worry, internalizing it instead. I didn't have any time to think during my heat, but I woke up clear-headed last night and watched these three as they slept. I took my time then to think everything through.

"I've made a decision about the job offer. Or offers, I guess." That gets their attention. Everyone sits at the table as Nick and

Colin fill plates with food and Kent serves drinks. They all stop and stare at me as if waiting to see if I'm going to attack.

"I wasn't going to accept the permanent job. I always intended to help with the renovations," I begin, watching their faces fall in disappointment. "But after I talked to Mama and we had our date that turned into a lot more, I've changed my mind."

Angry scowls replace the disappointment. They think I'm rejecting both offers. I hold up a hand before anyone can speak. "I'll happily take both jobs, if that's what you three really want. The renovation, I can handle in my sleep. The other, well, that's going to be more of a challenge. But provided you'll all be willing to help me learn, I'm in."

I stare between the three of them as it takes a minute for my words to sink in. Wow, for three smart guys, they really are being slow today. I start to eat my breakfast while I wait.

"You're taking the job? For real? This isn't a joke. You're coming to work with us," Nick says in shock.

"I knew you would," Colin winks at me. I don't argue with him, even though he looked just as disappointed and angry as the other two just a moment ago.

"That's wonderful news. I have some errands to attend to after breakfast, and I'll get the contract drawn up then as well." Kent seems colder and detached, as if he's pushing me away. I don't want to believe that, but I know it's possible he's regretting what happened between us.

"I also wanted to apologize for what I did. It was reckless and I shouldn't have done it. I'm sorry. I didn't mean to bind you to me without knowing it was what you wanted. I don't know if there's a way to undo it or not, but I hope you don't feel obligated because of it." I know it's immature, but I can't help it. I race up the stairs and shut myself in my nest. Everything is too much right now. I can't think straight. I fall onto the pile of pillows and let myself cry.

KENT

"That isn't good. Give her a few minutes, then check on her. Don't tell her where I've gone, just that I'll be back soon. I'll get what we need, and we'll handle this. Unless either of you has changed your minds?" I look from Nick to Colin. They both look terrified at Court's outburst. Does she think we're going to reject her?

"I won't change my mind. I'll clean up down here, then go check on her," Nick says quietly. It's odd to see the man who is never serious with a stoic expression.

"Me neither. I'll help Nick. You get everything together as quick as you can. She's going to need all three of us," Colin orders.

I give them each a quick kiss goodbye, promising to send pictures to get their input. I'm worried, but also certain we can get everything back on track.

Two hours later, I walk into a quiet house with the ring tucked carefully in my pocket. I know that Nick and Colin are trying to convince Court to come out of her nest, but she's not budging. I meet them outside her nest. "Let me talk to her for a second," I request, getting them to let me close to the door.

"Courtney, sweetheart, I know that you're upset. I respect your need for privacy, but we need to talk to you. Please open the door and let us in," I pose it as an order instead of a question. I don't know how she'll react, but I hope for the best.

A moment later, we hear the lock click. She's letting us in without opening the door. I ease it open, careful to move slowly since I'm not sure where she is. Once we're inside, I see her curled up in the center of the nest. The entire room still smells like the four of us. Memories of the past two days locked in here come back and my dick twitches.

I drop to my knees next to her, then watch as Colin and Nick do the same. "Sweetheart, please look at us. I'm sorry if we did or said something to upset you." It takes a minute, but she finally moves to meet my gaze.

"I shouldn't have claimed you without talking about it first." Her voice is shaky and it's obvious that she's been crying.

"No need to apologize. You just sped up our timeline, that's all. The three of us have been discussing this since you agreed to date us. We wanted to claim you. We just weren't sure how you felt about it until you claimed us first."

Her eyes open wide and she looks as if she's going to argue with me. Nick stops her. "He's not making that up. We were going to give you more time to decide, but your heat hit so suddenly."

"You are everything we've ever wanted. The three of us love each other, but we've always felt like something was missing," Colin adds.

COLIN

I take her hand and pull her out of the pillows. I'm sitting in front of her, with Kent and Nick on either side. "Do you mean that?" she asks quietly.

I press my lips to her forehead. "Yes, princess. We mean it. As a matter of fact, we have something for you." I look at Kent, silently asking him to take the lead on this. He shakes his head, looking at Nick. I nod, nudging Nick. Kent passes him the ring behind Courtney's back.

"Courtney, honey, I'm not really good at words, but here goes nothing." He takes a deep breath and continues. "You light up a room when you enter it. You make my heart smile just by being yourself. I know that I speak for all three of us when I say, we've fallen in love with you. Will you marry us?"

He opens the ring box and offers it to her. "What?" Her eyes go wide again and I can tell she wasn't expecting this.

"Well, Nick just told you that we love you, and asked if you'll marry us. I mean, come on, princess, he didn't even mutter this time." I can't help teasing her to help her relax. I know that she was caught off guard and needs a minute to think.

"I heard him, I'm just not sure what to say," she bites back at me. I can tell that she's not upset, though.

Kent kisses her cheek. "If it's too soon, we'll understand. No one will force you into anything. We just didn't want you to think we didn't want to claim and bond with you. Because that's all we want."

Tears fill her eyes, and I know that I'm in danger of losing control. I can't handle tears, and I'm not sure if these are happy or sad. After another minute or two, my heart starts racing and panic sets in.

"Princess? Please say something. I can't stand to see you cry," I admit. I can't take the waiting for her to decide our future.

"I'm sorry," she says, and I know she's rejecting us. She's decided that she regrets claiming us and being claimed by us. What changed in that small amount of time? I'm desperate to fix this, but I have no idea what we've done wrong.

I rub my hands over my face and back away from her. I can't stand to be here right now. I can't face her. Before I can leave the room, her hand clamps down on my arm. "Wait," she pleads. "I wasn't done. I'm sorry for overreacting and for the tears. I wasn't trying to manipulate anyone. I would love to marry you three. But only if that's what you truly want. I can't handle the thought that I've forced you into this."

Her tender words have tears falling from my eyes. She reaches up and brushes them away. "I love you. All of you."

NICK

Courtney holds her hand out to me as she drags Colin to her mouth and claims him with a kiss. I slide the ring on her finger easily, impressed that Kent got her size perfect. When she lets go of Colin, Court turns to Kent. He kisses her so tenderly that I feel tears of my own well up. I can't believe that she said yes. I wait patiently for her to turn to me. When she does, I pull her into my lap and press my lips gently to hers. I want to show her how much we cherish her. I pour every ounce of emotion into this kiss.

When she pulls away, I wipe her tears away with my thumbs, my hands framing her face. The three of us engulf her in a hug. I'm not sure there could have been a more perfect moment in our lives. "It's been a long day, and I'm sure you're exhausted. We can discuss details tomorrow and start planning the wedding," I offer. Kent rubs a hand up her back and Colin rests his hand on her thigh.

"As if I don't already have it all planned out," she laughs. I can't tell if she's serious or not. My eyes go wide and I look at Kent. He looks at Colin who shrugs.

"Well, if that's true, you can show us what you want tomorrow. Let's just enjoy being snuggled up tonight," Colin suggests.

"Can we order that pizza? We didn't get to finish our Valentine's Day date because of my heat. Dinner and a movie?" None of us could ever deny our omega what she desires.

Kent kisses her before going to order the pizza. Colin presses his lips to her forehead again. "I'll pick the movie. I know the perfect one." Then he's gone and it's just us.

"I thought you were going to say no." I hate the look she gives me at my admission. "I'm so glad you didn't, but I was terrified."

"I know. And I'm sorry. Everything today has just been too much to handle. I thought you guys were rejecting me when you weren't here this morning. I was prepared to say goodbye," she whispers. Fuck, how could I not have realized that was the problem all along?

"Oh, my sweet Court. I will never reject you. Neither will Kent or Colin. You're so good for us. You're helping Colin heal, and making Kent relax. This is the most themselves they've been since everything happened with Terri." I'm sure they'd get upset if they knew I told her that, but I don't care. She deserves to know how she affects us. And I refuse to hide anything from our omega. I can't wait to make her ours.

I won't ever tell her that Kent stretched the truth when he told her we'd discussed everything before. We'd barely thought to talk about claiming or heats before hers happened. Luckily, we all agreed that she was the one we wanted.

COURTNEY

Dinner and a movie is a success. I know that tomorrow, I'll have to call Mama and give her the news. Then we can sit back and watch as the gossip spreads around town. For once, I'm not worried about what Ms. Gertrude or Katie will say. I'm perfectly happy with my choice, and the only thing I'm concerned about is getting this wedding planned as soon as possible.

After the first movie, it's still early, so I insist we watch another. I sneak upstairs and grab my wedding binder. Kent's eyes go wide when he sees it. Clearly, he didn't believe me when I said I had it all planned out. I've already pulled the pages related to my dress out. It's bad luck for the groom or grooms to see the dress before the wedding.

I drop onto the couch with Kent on my right and Nick on my left. Colin sits in front of me on the floor, resting his arm on my knee. "Welcome to my wedding," I tell them, opening the book. We go through each page, carefully discussing each of my selections. It's obvious that they will agree to anything to make me happy, since some of the things I have in here are at least a decade old.

I know that we'll make some changes and compromise on a few things, but I enjoy teasing them about my super serious choices. We laugh and talk into the night. After we go through the entire binder, we settle in for the second movie. Halfway through, Colin is stretched across our laps, sleeping. Nick rests his head on my shoulder, and Kent holds my hand gently.

I can't stop staring at the gorgeous pink diamond ring they picked for me. What did I do to deserve these men? I say a silent thank you to the universe for small miracles. Out of nowhere, all of my dreams are coming true. A few minutes later, I hear soft snores coming from my left. Nick is asleep too.

I turn to Kent and notice that he's barely keeping his eyes open. "You tired?" He hums a response and leans his head on my shoulder. Suddenly, I'm the pillow for my pack, and I don't mind at all.

I know that not everything will be this easy, but I'm looking forward to taking each step with them. These amazing men came into my life when I doubted myself. They helped me see that I am worthy, no matter what other people said. I think about Nick's words from earlier. He says that I'm good for them. Maybe, but they're good for me. I can't wait to call Mama and tell her our wonderful news. And with most of the wedding plans done already, or just needing small tweaks, we should be able to get everything done by spring. I wonder if they're ready for this. I watch my men as they sleep, before I drift off with them.

What Next?

IF YOU ENJOYED THIS book, please consider writing a review. Indie authors, even those with indie publishers, can only thrive if word of their books gets out into the world. Reviews matter. They don't have to be overly detailed, just a sentence or two about what you enjoyed.

Thanks for reading!

About the Author

M.P. Starkweather is a wife, mother, author, poet, casual online gamer, self-proclaimed fan-girl, and full-time nerd. She writes free-form poetry, paranormal romance, sci-fi romance, reverse harem romance, and is branching out into contemporary romance. In her free time, she enjoys writing, reading, Dungeons & Dragons, table top games with her husband and friends, and playing with her son. M.P. also enjoys tv, movies, and music across various genres.

To get the most up-to-date information about her latest releases and book signings, check out www.mpstarkweather .com and join her newsletter, or follow her on your favorite social media site.

Also By M.P. Starkweather

Standalones - Contemporary RH OV

Cold Princes

Knot My Valentine

The Pack Next Door – Contemporary RH OV series

Princess or Knot

Fiancée or Knot

Queen or Knot

Vampires at Midnight - Paranormal RH series

Blood Moon

Blood Lost

Blood War

A Vampires at Midnight and Hunters of the Forest Crossover Novella - Paranormal RH, free with newsletter sign up

Blood Wolf

Hunters of the Forest - Paranormal RH series

Wolf Bane

Wolf Caged

Wolf Moon

The Legend of Khaine Academy – Paranormal RH Academy series
The Awakening (pre-order coming soon!)
Forged by Magic - Sci-fi/Fantasy M/F series

Hidden

Betrayed

Saved

Daydreams and Sunsets - a collection of poetry

<u>Daydreams and Sunsets</u>